With special thanks to Beatrice Puxley for kindly designing and creating the front cover of this book.

This book is dedicated to my mum Margaret for always supporting me, I've never met a more amazing woman.

I would also like to dedicate this book to my husband Chris for always being my biggest cheerleader and encouraging me to do anything I put my mind to.

WYNTER

My name is Wynter Jones, I was named after my mother's favourite season but with a "Y", just to be that little bit different. Just like my name everything about my life is different, my mother gave birth to me in the back of a taxicab at 19 years old, that's different, I have one green eye and one blue eye, that's different, I have a birthmark on my lower back that is shaped like a perfect heart, that's different and I act as both a sister and a mother to my two younger siblings Alma and Cleo, that's different, but I'll come back to that later. The story that I am about to tell you is so incredible that if I wasn't there I'd have struggled to believe it really happened, but it did happen, pinkie swear and you can never break a pinkie swear, so I guess I will just start from the beginning.

I had been walking the same road every single day since I was about five years old, down the long dirt road behind my house, with every press of my old tattered trainers into the ground, they would sink, leaving the imprint of my sole in the soil and engulfing them in even more filth than was already covering them but it didn't matter how dirty they got, my mother couldn't afford new ones so I would just have to make do. I'd make my way through the little village of Bainville that ran to the side of the town where I lived, Sherwood, and to the modest little convenience store "Polly's Pocket" that sat perched, looking over the dock below where fishermen often came to fuel up or grab a quick snack, it wasn't the closest one to where I lived but most people who lived in Sherwood dreamed of getting out and that 3 and a half mile walk was the closest I would ever get. That particular evening there was a frosty bite in the air, it nipped at my fingers as they retreated into the sleeve of my paper-thin cardigan I paused in my tracks, turning my attention to the sky, where the sun had begun meeting the moon as the sky was beginning to turn from a crisp blue to a darker version of its earlier self. I could see my breath as it filled the air like a deep smoke so thick for a moment it clouded my vision, I stepped inside the store for warmth.

"Good Evening Wynter, the usual?"
Polly Proctor was the owner of the store and had been for as long as I could remember, she was petite, only a little bit taller than me and I was 11, She was in her thirties but looked much older, her elbows stuck out like wings as she stood uncomfortably behind the cash register and her hairline had begun to recede but I put that down to the fact her husband had left her when she was pregnant with her daughter, life truly had dealt her a crappy hand, she had inherited the store from her late mother, it wasn't her dream but she had settled, at least, that's what she told me.

"Yes, thank you Miss Proctor"
"Wynter, I've told you before, Miss Proctor was my mother, Polly is fine..."
Polly handed me a loaf of bread, white, no crusts, a carton of milk, semi-skimmed and three chocolate coins, I didn't ask for the chocolate coins but she always gave them to me anyway, I placed the money on the counter, all small change and stood patiently as Polly counted it out.

"You're a little short today Wynter"
"I'm sorry Mrs Proctor, I mean,, Polly, it's all I have, I must have miscounted" I didn't miscount, I knew exactly how much I had and how much I needed, but our cupboards were bare and my sisters were counting on me. Polly thought for a moment.

"Since it's you, I'll let you off"
I smiled gratefully and she gave me a wink before I grabbed the bread in one hand and the milk in the other,

slipped the chocolate coins into my pocket and left without another word.

Sherwood was a small town that was tucked in the back corner of North Carolina, so small that if you were driving through it and you blinked, you'd miss it, It was mostly green, for miles and miles and if you tasted the air it tasted like freshly cut grass, on one side it was known for its white picket fences and upper class suburban homes and on the other side was where I lived, stood small bungalows that had seen better days and a forgotten old park that had been there for at least a decade that now had overgrown weeds and flaking paint work. In the entirety of my 11 years residing in Sherwood, nothing exciting ever happened, everyone just seemed to go on with their ordinary boring lives, including me.

They called me Wild Wynter because most of the time I looked like I had been dragged through a bush backwards but also because I just did my own thing, kept to myself and danced to the beat of my own drum, but they didn't know my story, very few did. I had to grow up pretty fast, my mother spent most of her time drunk, about to get drunk or recovering from being drunk, that is when she didn't have one of her boyfriends over, I didn't know their names so I addressed them by numbers, boyfriend number 1 was super quiet and mysterious, a policeman my mother had picked up on a night out to get herself out of being arrested for a reason I still don't know, boyfriend number 2 looked kind of like a pug, mama really was wearing her beer goggles when she picked that one out, boyfriend number 6 was my least favourite, he gave me creepy vibes and when he was around I'd barricade myself in my room until I was sure he had left in the morning and boyfriend number 17, the most recent, well I'm pretty sure he shared a braincell with a chimpanzee and he didn't get the intelligent part. My mother wasn't a bad person, she just made bad choices and most of the time I was left to pick up the pieces.

When I got home the door was unlocked, we lived in a small compact bungalow a stone's throw away from the town centre, it was unassuming and had been needing a paint job for at least 5 years, but it was home and had been for a lot of my life. As soon as I pushed open the door, the intoxicating fumes smacked me like a tonne of bricks, it was always the worst when you first entered but you got used to it after a while, Our house reeked of the stench of alcohol mixed with cigarette smoke and whatever meal my mother had burned in the oven that day. I ventured into the living room, my mother was asleep on the couch hugging a glass bottle that I could only assume once held beer, a pile of dirty clothes lay on the floor next to her combined with empty bottles, tissues and remnants of food. My home didn't feel very homely, the floor was only half carpeted, the other half was bare wood, you know, the stuff that was usually under the carpet, from a time my mother had friends over and long story short, it got ruined, there was cracks in the foundations of almost every single wall and there was a distinct lack of framed family pictures throughout the house and no artwork on the fridge. The kitchen was attached to the living room and its state wasn't much better, there was a mountain of unwashed dishes sitting in the sink and the worktops were stained and chipped and don't get me started on the distinct lack of anything edible.

"Wynie, Wynie!" My younger sister, Alma, the middle child, came bounding out of the kitchen at full speed like a race car in the grand prix, losing control as she tripped on a baked beans can on the floor that had been there for god knows how long, I grabbed her briskly and silenced her by placing my hand over her mouth, at first she tried to struggle out of my grip but once she spotted our mother on the couch, she put the pieces together in her head and relaxed her body in my arms, I handed her the bread and milk and ordered her to put it in the kitchen whilst I made my way to our bedroom, if you could call it that. Myself and my two sisters slept on one single mattress in the middle of the bedroom floor that we shared, it was a box room, no bigger than the average cupboard, the walls were not papered and mould had started growing in the corner near the door but my mother didn't work and she drank away any money she did get so I was grateful for a roof over our heads. My youngest sister, Cleo was lying on her back on the mattress kicking her little chubby legs and grabbing her feet with her hands, I scooped her up into my arms, she was wet and whimpering.

"Looks like you need a change" I rested her down on a folded bath towel that I had retrieved from the bathroom and placed on the floor, we were all out of diapers so I used one of my old T-shirts that I had outgrown. "There, much better"
I kissed Cleo on the head and sat down with her as Alma joined us. Alma was small for her age; people often mistook her for a toddler when she was in fact 5 years old. Her skin carried a subtle warmth, like sun-kissed sand, with big round amber coloured eyes filled with curiosity and wonder, her hair was a cascade of caramel waves that went down to the centre of her back and formed in natural ringlets from the moment she woke up in the morning to the moment she went to bed, a feature I was very jealous of. When Alma looked at the world it was as if she was taking in every single detail. She was very calm and mature beyond her years, she had always been that way, even as an infant, quite the opposite of Cleo, "chaotic Cleo"" I often called her, she had quite a temper for her

tiny little frame, once she saw red, there was no stopping the inevitable melt down that was going to come. Cleo and Alma couldn't look more different, if you saw them together you wouldn't even think they were related, Cleo's hair was very fine and fiery red like burning embers, her eyes were the colour of the sky on a sunny day and much like myself she was as pale as freshly fallen snow.
    "Wynter I'm hungry" Alma complained, clutching her stomach with both hands.
    "Well, I have a surprise for you... Close your eyes" Alma scrunched up her face as she closed her eyes and I reached my hand into my pocket and pulled out the chocolate coins that I had received from Polly. I reached my hand out to her holding the coin in my palm.
    "Open your eyes Ally cat"
Alma's face lit up like the sun rising from the darkness.
    "Can I eat it?"
    "Of course you can"
Alma tentatively took one of the coins from my hand as if she was worried it might disappear, unwrapped it and took a bite, savouring every mouthful, I unwrapped one for Cleo broke off a bit and she took it in her hand, smiling, she was still innocent, she hadn't been tainted by life yet, and I intended to keep it that way, I cradled her in my arms as she burrowed her head into my neck, she was warm, like a breathing water bottle, I hoped to protect her for the rest of her life, so that she would never see some of the things that I had seen.

    Every night before bed Alma, Cleo and I would sit by the window that overlooked the overgrown forest that when I was younger, I used to think was haunted, counting the trees as they danced in the wind, wondering if they had any thoughts, any feelings, a strategy I'd use to distract them from the rabble that often came from the living room when our mother had friends over, men friends in particular. I could hear the glasses chinking, the music booming, the people stumbling, I could always hear it, I placed my hands gently over Cleo's ears.

"Alright Alma, bedtime"

"Just five more minutes, please"

"I already gave you five more minutes, bed, now" I ordered her sternly.

Alma rolled her eyes and climbed down from the windowsill and onto the mattress, I placed Cleo down next to her and pulled the thin blanket up to their chins.

"Night night, sleep tight, don't let the bed bugs bite"

"Bed bugs?! I don't want them to bite me!"

"It's just a little rhyme Alma, close your eyes and go to sleep, I'll be right here."

Slowly but surely, Cleo and Alma drifted off to sleep but I stayed awake, I always stayed awake until I was sure that everyone had left, to keep them safe. 03:32AM, the house finally fell silent and I allowed myself to float off to sleep.

Weekday mornings were always the hardest, I'd wake up with the sun at 6AM, creep through the living room where my mother slept to tidy up from the night before, at 6.30 I'd wake Cleo up, change her and give her a bottle of milk, I'd wake Alma up last, at 7PM, she was not a morning person and it normally took a few tries and even when she finally was awake she wasn't ready for any form of conversation and we'd leave bang on 7:30PM. I'd drop Cleo off at the child minder who lived three doors down from us and Alma to her school before making my way to my own school, I was always early, but it was better than being late.

I was kind of somewhere in between a loner and a social butterfly, I liked to be around other people, performing, making people laugh but on the other hand I just wanted to be alone, to hide under a rock and never come out, maybe be invisible.

"Hey Summer!"

Every day it was a different season, everyone thought it was hilarious because my name was Wynter but I'd heard it my whole life so it was getting old.

"Wow Genevieve, you think of that one all by yourself?"

"Geez, did someone spit in your cornflakes?"

I hadn't had cornflakes, I had two slices of an old orange that I shared with my two siblings.

"Something like that..."

Genevieve Paxton and I had a love hate relationship, she was the only person in the school who knew my situation, I spent a lot of time at her house when I was younger to get away from home but in all honestly, she was the human equivalent of a headache most of the time. Genevieve was short in stature but she was mighty and feisty in personality, not a person to get on the bad side of, her hair was auburn, the colour of fire, much like her nature and her eyes were sapphire blue. The only reason I kept her around was because she was a good person to have on your side, she'd fight tooth and nail for you if someone other than her came after you. Second in line to Genevieve's throne was Riley Daniels, Riley was the daughter of Sherwood's most successful family lawyer, Darwin Daniels, which made sense because she liked to argue about anything and everything, if you said the sky was blue, she'd argue it was green and she'd have you convinced that you were wrong. Riley was half Chinese half Korean with short jet black hair that curled in just under her chin and tree trunk brown eyes, she was arguably one of the smartest people in my class, if not the entire school, and last but not least was Orla Grey, most of the time she barely said a word, just stood there with her arms crossed over her chest looking unimpressed with the world, Orla was tall, way taller than most girls my age, her hair was white blonde, often straightened down to the end of her spine, she was on every school sports team that ever existed, cross country, netball, handball, you name it, she was on it and she excelled at it.

"You get dressed in the dark today Wynter?" Genevieve caught up to me as I walked passed her.

"You get dressed at all today G? Cause that skirts so short I can almost see what you ate for breakfast, pancakes was it?"

"Touché... So did you get it done?"

"Don't I always?"

I reached into my old tattered backpack that I had picked up in the Charity shop in town a year earlier and handed Genevieve the folder that I had prepared a few nights before. Inside the folder was the homework expected by our Maths teacher that day, I liked to think of it as my little business, students would pay me and in return I would do their homework for them, it was my way of making a little extra money to pay for the food that we needed that my mother couldn't afford to buy.

"What did I get?"

"B-"

"That's it?"

"You're a B student G, if I gave you an A, Miss Larkin would get suspicious... you're welcome"

The front entrance to Sherwood Elementary reminded me of a prison, dark and depressing with swing doors painted in jet black paint with silver metal handles, it had been remodelled a few years before I even went there but if you ask me, it looked way better before, inside was the polar opposite to the outside, it was juvenile, with hand painted fairies and mythical creatures like dragons and unicorns painted all the way down the hallway, on the left the whole way down the hallway were our lockers, painted in all of the colours of the rainbow, my locker was at the furthest point in entire school and right next to the boys bathroom, so I enjoyed the faint smell of urine and... Other things, whilst collecting my books for the day, lovely.

During class, I liked to fly under the radar, I knew all the answers but never put my hand up when the teacher asked questions, when we needed partners for assignments I waited to see who hadn't been chosen at the end and just went with them, I kind of just faded into the background. My seat was by the window and the high school track team practiced in our school yard so most of the time I'd gaze out the window as they ran around the gravel track, today was no different, I watched as they ran round and round and round until I was brought out of my gaze by Miss Larkin asking the square route of A.

"Wynter Jones, you're smarter than this, please pay attention"

"Sorry Miss"

"What's the answer then?"

"The square route of A is 4"

School finished at 3PM, firstly I'd sprint to meet Alma by the gates of her school before we both walked to collect Cleo from the child minder for 3:15. The child minder, Caroline Warner, a 21 year old college dropout from Canada, lived three houses down from us in a little wooden bungalow that she had inherited from her grandmother with her two rat like dogs Ollie and Quinnie. She was standing at the door when we arrived, chewing gum with her mouth open, gross.

"C'mon little lamb, your sisters here to pick you up." I heard her say as she scooped Cleo into her arms, though Cleo didn't look best pleased, her eyes were puffy like she'd been crying and what very little hair she had was standing straight up at the top of her head, she reached for me on approach, her little chubby hands grabbing the air. Cleo showed no sign of wanting to learn how to speak, in fact, unless she was crying or whining, she barely made a sound at all.

"How was she?" I asked as Cleo dived into my arms head first, so harshly that I almost dropped her on her face.

"She's been fine up until the last hour or so, she got a bit cranky, didn't you" Caroline pinched Cleo's cheeks, Cleo was unimpressed and retreated further into my arms with that little pouty face she made when she didn't get her own way.

"Well, thanks again Caroline" I reached into my back pocket, pulled out the money and thrusted it into her hand.

"How's your mama?"

"Yeah, she's doing well" I lied, I hadn't seen my mother awake in three days "she works a lot though so it's just easier for me to collect Cleo", another lie, my mother hadn't held down a job since I was 4 years old when she worked nightshift at some 24 hour diner, she said she was fired because her manager was sexist, but I knew it was because she stole from the till on a daily basis. Sometimes it was easier to lie than deal with the plague of questions that came along with the truth, I had been conditioned from a young age to tweak the narrative to suit the situation and honestly, I wasn't sure if it was a good thing or a bad thing. I took Alma by the hand and we walked the short distance to our home.

"Alma, take Cleo into the bedroom" I passed Cleo onto Alma and patted her back as she made her way to our little bedroom, we weren't alone in the house, it was deafeningly quiet but I knew we weren't on our own. I kicked my shoes off and crept barefoot through the living room over the shredded cheese puff crumbs, damp patches from spilled beer and shells of nuts.

"Louis, stop!" The whisper came from a room that stemmed just off the living room, a room we never used, where we kept the vacuum and the laundry basket that never got used, the door was ajar but only by a crack, I couldn't stop my feet from walking until I was standing directly outside, peering into the darkness, I could see the back of my mother wrapped up in a man that I didn't recognise, he was tall and lanky with limbs like branches off of trees, his eyes, or what I saw of them, seemed vacant, he looked up, oh no, we locked eyes, crap.

"Who's this?" The man unlatched himself from my mother and turned his attention to me. "What's your name?" He opened the door revealing me like a prize in one of those game shows my mother was always watching, though I tried so hard to remain hidden, he crouched down to me in the patronizing way most adults did with kids, in a way that made me want to kick him in the shins, but I refrained from doing so.

"Don't mind her Louis" My mother rolled her eyes motioning for me to leave but my feet were glued to the floor, my voice box unable to speak.

"You didn't tell me you had a kid Lyric"

"Wynter will go to her room, it'll be like she's not even here, the kid is practically a grown up anyway"
My mother acted like I wasn't there, most of the time anyway, so this was no different.

"If you'd have said you had a kid I'd... I'm not ready for this man, sorry"
The man called Louis backed away from my mother like she had just told him she was an alien from another planet as she walked towards him and then he turned to leave, she ran after him screaming his name, right out onto the

sidewalk, I followed.

"Louis! Louis!" She fell to her knees and bowed her head I could hear the stifled wails as she covered her mouth with her hand. Every. Single. Time. None of my mother's male friends stuck around, they always found a reason to leave, I was starting to think that I wasn't the problem after all, maybe it was her, maybe they could see though her facade, maybe they could sense the chaos that was her own mind. Tentatively I approached her, people were staring as they passed, craning their necks to glare, I could practically read their minds as they shook their heads and walked off, but it wasn't the first time my mother had broken down in the street, there was the time boyfriend number 9, the bartender with the unibrow broke up with her because he wanted "to just be friends" and there was the time she didn't get the job at the restaurant in town because she dressed too provocatively, I couldn't get her out of bed for a week after that one, I rested a gentle hand on her back.

"Mama, I'm sorry, please come back inside."

"This is all your fault!" She grabbed my wrist like she could squeeze right through to the bone, stood up and began to march me back inside, like a Sargent in the army, focussed, determined to make it to her destination, slamming the door behind her so hard I thought it might shatter into a million tiny pieces, all the while she didn't let go of my arm.

"Mama, I_" Smack, I felt the sting of her palm connecting with my face, my mother never hit me, only threatened it, we were both shocked, standing in silence for a moment just staring at one another my hand on my cheek in an attempt to stop the aching, it didn't help. Alma was standing in the door way to our bedroom, gaped at the mouth, tear-stained cheeks, her tiny body trembling.

"I'm so sorry Wynter" I knew she was, she was

always sorry, but she never changed, so was she really sorry, or was that just another empty statement?

No matter how much I tried that night Alma just wouldn't go to sleep, she just wanted to snuggle into me and have me read to her, the same story, over and over again, Cleo was restless too, whimpering and moaning as I rocked her in my arms, sometimes I wished I was a baby again, ignorant to the world, no responsibilities, no pressures, nobody expected anything of you. Cleo wrapped her hand around my pinkie finger and looked up at me with her big blue longing eyes.

"It's okay, I've got you baby girl, I won't let anything happen to you, I promise" I wasn't sure if she could understand me or not, sometimes it felt like she knew exactly what I was saying and other times it felt like I was talking to a brick wall but that night it seemed like she understood because she held my finger tighter and the corner of her lips pulled upwards into a smile like she knew I needed it. Alma wrapped herself underneath my one free arm and draped her arms around my waist as if it was her only means of survival.

"Wynter" she started, her voice shaking "why does mama hate us?"

"She doesn't hate us Alma..." I didn't think she did anyway "Mama's just... She's sick"

"Is she going to die?"

"No, not physically sick, but inside her head... She needs help, so we need to go easy on her okay? She's a good person"

"how does she get the help?"

"She has to want it"

"Why doesn't she want it"

"Well, sometimes, Alma, people don't always know they're sick"

"We should tell her"

"It's not that simple"
I knew Alma was too young to understand what I was trying to say but I hoped maybe one day it would sink in.

PEYTON

My bed was always the most comfortable when it was time to get up for work, I didn't hate my job, quite the opposite actually, I looked forward to it every day but on the mornings where the air was brisk and the windows were steamed up with condensation, I could have used at least another hour of shut eye. I worked as a teacher at Sherwood Elementary school and had done since I graduated from University two years prior, my class was the 5th grade, a bunch of pre-pubescent, attitude driven crazy kids, but I loved them for it. I took a deep breath and swung both of my legs over the side of the bed and rested my bare feet on the ice-cold wooden floor, as I did I could hear a faint babbling from the room next door to mine.

"Penny, mamas coming!"

When I entered to room, my 2-year-old daughter was standing upright in her crib, her blonde hair sticking up like static on top of her head, beaming with a sort of joy that you definitely lose as you get older. I scooped her up into my arms, planted a kiss on her forehead and began to get her ready. I got married young, at 18, much to my parents dismay to a 21-year-old artist from Manhattan, Overnight I moved from the small, sleepy town of Sherwood where I grew up to the bustling chaos of New York City, with the man of my dreams, his name was Bailey, tall and mysterious yet fun loving and goofy, he truly was the perfect mould. Three years after we got married and 5 days after my graduation, I found out I was pregnant with our first and only child, a girl, he insisted on the name Penelope Joy Larkin, Penny for short, it was his late grandmothers name and he wanted to honour her. 5 months into my pregnancy I was waiting at home for my husband to arrive home from the art class he was teaching so that we could go out to dinner to celebrate his birthday that was coming up 2 days later, I had been feeling very emotional that day, the pregnancy hormones had been hitting me hard, or maybe I could sense what was coming. I remembered that day well, I was sitting at my vanity fixing my hair into a bun and doing my makeup when all of a sudden there was a knock at the door, maybe Bailey had forgotten his keys, why else would he knock? I smiled silently to myself, rolled my eyes and made my way for the door, I unhooked the securing chain and opened it but it wasn't Bailey, it was two men, uniformed police officers.

"Peyton Larkin?"

I nodded my head sheepishly, was Bailey in trouble?, was he hurt?

"Peyton, I am officer Martin Gibson and this is Officer Simon Clark, your husband, Bailey, he was in a car accident."

My heart thudded to the pit of my stomach, I felt physically sick.

"Where is he, is he hurt?" I managed, though I feared that I already knew the answer.

"Mrs Larkin..."

I collapsed to my knees and began to wail. Bailey had been pronounced dead at the scene after a head on collision with a truck. 3 weeks after the funeral I up and left the big city to move back to my small town of Sherwood, by then both my parents had passed on and my sister had moved to West Virginia for her job but it still felt like home, for me, it felt like the safest place in the world a place where no one knew my story, a place I could start again.

After dropping Penny off with her sitter I headed for work. My classroom was the smallest in the school, but I made the most of it with brightly colour letters scattered over the walls, the Christmas artwork that the children did was still up but it was the first day back after the break so I hadn't had the chance to take it down.

"Morning Peyton..." Lara Giles was my main companion, we were the two youngest teachers so it was only natural that we tended to band together.

"Hey!" I exclaimed pulling the giant hand drawn Christmas tree from the wall and wrapping all different colours of tinsel around some cardboard to store in the supply closet.

"Should you really be up that ladder without someone here?" Lara laughed as she stuck her foot on the bottom step of the ladder.

"Probably not." I shrugged now picking off the line of crafted penguins. "How was your Christmas?"

"same old same old, you?"

"Yeah really good thanks." I said, knowing fine well I spent it alone, the bell rang interrupting our conversation, I climbed down the ladders, chucked them in the supply closet and opened the door.

"Good Morning Miss..." One by one a sea of 11-year-olds plagued my classroom, taking their seats, rabbling like they hadn't seen one another for years I smiled to myself, this was the life. Last to enter, a young girl, small in stature, slightly hunched over, seemingly uncomfortable like she just wanted to blend in, but I noticed her. Her name was Wynter Jones and although quiet, she was silently intelligent, arguable the most so in the whole class but she never put her hand up to answer any questions, never finished her assessments first and spent most of the day staring out the window onto the playground, but she never achieved less than 100 on any of her tests and whenever I asked her anything she knew the answer, she was peculiar.

"Alright class, please have your homework displayed on your desk for me to pick up."

These were the moments you could separate the underperformers from everyone else, the panicked expressions on their faces, the fiddling of their hands, the looking around to see if anyone else was in their position, I could tell who had done nothing all break. Dominic Stanton, never did his homework but I knew his workaholic mother was not enforcing it at home, Clare Bryony, she was always a hit or miss, she was a very much "on my terms" kind of person, she didn't struggle in class but she was inconsistent with her homework, Max Styler, now that boy was a terror.

"Thank you, thank you" I spoke enthusiastically as I weaved in and out of desks collecting their folders. "Max, no homework again?"

"Dog ate it." Max shrugged, you're not supposed to hit children or even think about it, especially when you're a teacher, but that was one child who deserved a good slap to knock him down a peg or two.

"Mr Styler, you may think that I was born yesterday but I do know every trick in the book, that homework better be on my desk by Friday or there's a weeks' worth of detention with your name on it..."
The rest of the class sniggered as I made my way back to the desk.

"Alright everyone, maths books out." I heard a unanimous groan that soon silenced as I tuned back around to face them. "We're going to do a pop quiz..."
I liked to keep them on their toes, never let them know your next move. I grabbed a hold of the chalkboard and slowly flipped it around displaying equations that I had come up with.

"Sasha, question A, what is the value of X"
Sasha Bevan was a shy girl, popular, everyone liked her but most of the time it felt like she was holding back. She stroked her chin like she had an imaginary beard, I could

see the clogs turning in her brain.

"8"

"Correct, Dominic, question B, complete the equation..."

"No idea" Dominic shrugged, I knew he did though, he just didn't want to look uncool in front of his boys.

"Maybe you'll know it from detention" Dominic straightened up in his chair, obviously conflicted. "Want to try again?"

"X= 9.7"

"Good job... Alright, last one..." I scanned the room watching as almost a of my students eyes darted around, avoiding eye contact. My eyes fell on Wynter Jones, her mind, seemingly in a far off place. "Wynter, question C... What is the square route of A?"
Wynter gazed out the window by her desk, in a trance fixated on something, anything other than school work. Wynter was pale, her dark eyes heavy as lead, like she hadn't slept in weeks, her clothes were never dirty but they were never clean either and her hair was often unbrushed, I wondered if her parents worked a lot and just didn't have time, if her mother worked two jobs to make ends meet and her dad had to work late, or the worse, more likely scenario. She was always so inside her own head that she barely ever seemed to be in reality with the rest of us, I'd have given anything to know what was going on inside her head...

"Wynter Jones, the square route of A...?

"Sorry Miss"

"What's the answer then?"

"The square route of A is 4"

The bell rang right on time at the end of the day, you'll never see anyone moving as fast as children when that high pitched piercing bell is sounded meaning that they can go home.

"Alright guys safe journey home and I'll see you bright and breezy tomorrow morning."
Within two seconds the classroom was empty, all barre me.

Everyday after class, I'd meet Lara in her art classroom to help her with some whacky idea she'd have for the students, today was no different. The art class was a place where kids could go to get away, it was set up in memory of a 13-year-old who sadly passed away, Bees Becket, I didn't know her but there wasn't one teacher in Sherwood elementary school who hadn't heard of her.

"So what is the point of this?"
"Pey, use your imagination, it's cats in space..."
"But why?"
"Why not?"

She had me there... There were many times I had wished I could be more like Lara, she never took anything too seriously, she was a free spirit was always laughing and just seemed to know what she wanted out of life and how to get it, I on the other hand, had no idea.

"Hey can I ask you something?"
"uh oh, that sounds serious..."
"Do you know Wynter Jones?"
"Everyone knows Wynter Jones, ask any of the teachers who've had her before you... Apparently she's practically a child genius..."
"What about her home life?"
"She walks past my house once a week to get things from the shop, I always wondered, maybe her mama is sick?"
"I'm not too sure, she just always seems to be spaced out, yet still paying attention somehow, she looks tired."

I picked a glue stick out of the box and stuck a cat onto the galaxy backdrop that Lara had painted, maybe I was over reacting, like usual, my mother always did say I was a drama queen.

"Peyton..." Lara placed her hand on top of mine gently and comfortingly "I know you worry about them, but you can't rescue every child..."

"Would you have rescued her if you could?"
I nodded towards the black and white picture of a young girl on a banner above the door, Bees Beckett was killed at the hands of her mothers new boyfriend, that's all I knew but It seemed to cut Lara deep, even today.

"That's different..." She stared lovingly up at the picture then back to me "I promise, if there's something wrong, you'll know..."

I spent that night lying in my bed awake, thinking about Wynter, I didn't know her very well, she was my only student I hadn't figured out all the way, she was an enigma but I was good with puzzles and I didn't know it yet but, I was about to fall head first into a whirlwind that I was not ready for.

WYNTER

When I was six years old my grandmother gifted me a snow globe for Christmas, inside was a mother bear and a baby bear, the baby bear clinging to its mother like a monkey to a tree, I wondered if there was a daddy bear or a sister bear or if it was just mother and baby trying to navigate through life, like myself and my mother, for the first 6 years of my life it was just the two of us, we were close, in an unconventional way, she didn't take me to the park to play on the swings or snuggle up on the couch and watch a movie with me, in fact, she needed me more than I needed her, to sing her to sleep when she was having an episode, to make food for her when she was glued to the couch, unwilling to move for days on end, most of the time it was just a sandwich of some sort but the thought was there, but she was my mother and I loved her with all of my heart. I protected that globe with my life, polishing it daily, shaking it and watching the snow fall down onto the figures and when my grandmother died it became my most prized possession, it sat on the small round table in the corner of our bedroom, no one was allowed to touch it though Alma and I would often sit and watch it when we couldn't sleep.

"Can we shake the globe?" She'd ask with pleading eyes her hands clasped prepared to beg if need be and I'd nod and we'd sit before it witnessing the blizzard, both wondering if, like the two bears inside the globe, we were also in the eye of the storm with no way out.

I rolled off the side of the mattress leaving Alma asleep, spread out fully across almost the entire surface like always, leaving me with barely any room, but I didn't mind. Cleo was already awake and had managed to manoeuvre her way to the bedroom door and sat herself in front of it, like a puppy dog wanting to go out. I picked her up under her arms and made my way to the kitchen, warmed up a bottle and fed it to her, her eyes seemed heavy, like she was tired but was too afraid to sleep in case she missed something, my mother was nowhere to be seen, she could disappear for days on end, those were the days I could breathe, the pressure wasn't so intense, I could just exist, I was never too sure what she would do during that time but I didn't really want to know. I didn't have to be as quiet when she wasn't around, in fact, I kind of liked it. Cleo pushed the bottle away from her mouth in an attempt to tell me she was finished and I put the rest in the fridge for later and sat her on the counter to give me a moments freedom to make the lunches for the day, I glanced at the clock, 6:34AM. Most of the time groceries were scarce so I would gather what little we had and try to make something out of it, we had bread and a banana so I crushed the banana and spread it onto the bread to make a sandwich but there was only enough for half a sandwich, I sealed each in a zip lock bag I also added a cocktail sausage, 3 M&M's each and half a KitKat placing the contents into brown paper bags ready for lunch. Alma was awakened with the early morning sun bang on 7.15 but didn't stumble out of the room until 7.30, her eyes squinting, half asleep, it was always the same, we never differed from the programme, sometimes I wondered how different things would be if I was born into another family. By 7.45 we were on our way.

It was the middle of winter but still the sun split the sky, it made you feel like you could wear shorts and a t-shirt but the wind was cold enough to break right through your skin and to your bones, as I held Alma's hand on the way to her school I could feel her trembling in my grip.

"Who lives there Wynter?" She pointed to the house in the corner of the street, it was different to all of the other houses on the street, for the longest time I thought it was haunted.

"I'm not sure, some old guy"
Everyone called him the hermit, you barely ever saw him and when you did, he often kept his head hung low, almost as if he didn't want to be seen. It was clear that he didn't want anyone in as he had constructed a double fence around his property and the gate was padlocked but everyone just ignored the weird behaviour because it had become normal over the years. Sometimes there was a girl, about my age, she sat by the gate, playing, I wondered who she was and wanted to introduce myself but was too afraid I'd be possessed by the haunted hermits house.

"And who's that girl?"

"I don't know Alma, now come on, we're going to be late"
Before I could even say another word Alma had taken her tiny little legs and strolled across the street, I ran after her, she was a girl on a mission making a bee line for the creepy house on the corner.

"Alma, wait" I finally caught up to her grabbing her forearm with my hand in an attempt to slow her down. "You cannot just walk off like that!"
She sighed pulling her arm from my grip, I wondered where this new attitude was coming from, Alma had never sassed me before.

"I just wanted to say hi to the girl"

"Alma, you don't know her and we don't talk to strangers remember?"

"She's a kid Wynter, how dangerous can she be?"
I took her hand and we continued down the street. If I am being completely honest, the house gave me the creeps, it made my blood run cold and my heart pound and I wasn't

about to charge into unknown territory like they do in those horror movies, but I was intrigued, about the girl, who she was, what her name was, why I hadn't seen her around school, was she home schooled, socially anxious? Just plain odd? I had so many questions that they were burning a hole in my brain.

"Wynter, your answer."

"Huh?"

"Wynter, I don't think the answer you're looking for is out that window"

I hadn't realised it but I hadn't been listening, in fact I felt like I was anywhere else but the classroom and now Miss Larkin was towering over me, arms crossed, eyebrows furrowed, how was I going to get out of this one? Miss Larkin was in her early 20's her hair was dark, almost black, like Snow White, her eyes were equally as dark and I was pretty sure if you looked too far into them she could see right into your soul and that terrified me.

"Sorry Miss"

"Again Wynter?, this is the second time this has happened, please don't make a habit of it."

I certainly wasn't about to make a habit of it, I hated the attention and just wanted the ground to swallow me whole. She offered one final stern look before retreating to the front of the class, I could hear the giggling from Genevieve and her minions at the back of the classroom, they sat together in a row, always whispering amongst themselves, about everyone, no one was safe, I was used to it by now though and I gave as good as I got most of the time. Our peace was shattered by a knock at the door following the skuttling of Miss Dalton, the school secretary, through the door, sometimes, I was sure that she thought she was the Principal, the way she carried herself, the way she acted, it bothered me slightly, but she was pretty harmless, she handed a note to Miss Larkin who read it and looked up, who was in trouble? Who's Granma died? Who had a doctor's appointment after school? Who was the lucky duck being bailed out of this prison early?

"Wynter, Mrs Holden wants to see you in her office, take your things" Miss Larkin announced, I grabbed my belongings and headed for the door running through the scenarios in my head of why I was being called to the principal's office.

Mrs Holden was a frightening women, the kind you'd see in your nightmares, I had never been sent to her office, what if she'd found out about my little side business? What if I was being suspended? My brain ticked over like a bomb ready to explode at any minute. The school hallway seemed much longer when you were riddled with anxiety. The door to Mrs Holden's office had been painted pale blue, she said she wanted it to seem welcoming, I wasn't sure if she had succeeded in that as I sheepishly knocked on the wood, so lightly I didn't think she'd even heard, but she had.

"Come in Wynter" How did she know it was me, I mean I know she had asked for me but still, it was like the woman could see through walls.
Hesitantly I pushed the door back on its hinges and entered her office, the outside may have appeared welcoming but the inside was not, the window on the far side of the room was so small it let barely any light in and the walls were covered in murky red wallpaper with black roses etched into them which didn't help as it made the room look like Draculas' layer. Mrs Holden sat in her big leather spinning chair that swallowed her whole, she was a small woman, shrivelled up and old, I mean, she was in her late 60's at least but for some reason she refused to retire. She motioned for me to sit down in the white plastic, less grand chair that sat on the other side of her desk, I did.

"The office received a phone call from your mother Wynter" She paused, oh no this wasn't good "A rather frantic phone call, that's the third one this week and it's only Thursday" She couldn't see me but I was clasping my hands so tightly under the desk that my knuckles were turning white and my fingers were turning red, almost the same colour I imagined by cheeks were flushing. "Is everything alright at home Wynter?" Mrs Holden tapped her long pink talon-like nails on the desk, looking over her round gold framed glasses at me.

"Everything is fine, at home, Mrs Holden."

"Are you sure? You know you can talk to me about anything, this is a safe place"
I hated when adults did that, patronise me, I wanted to yell in her face to back off, but I didn't I just nodded.

"Well..." She started, sighing, like she knew she couldn't get me to crack "She wants you to pick your sisters up early and go straight home"

I ran as fast as I possibly could to Alma's school to check her out and then on to pick Cleo up from Caroline's. When I got home my mother was there, sitting on the couch, her head in her hands, rocking back and forth, the last time I had saw her like that was just after Cleo was born and she was shocked that her body hadn't just bounced back to its natural state, I handed Cleo off to Alma and sent them into the bedroom before sitting myself down next to my mother, I could hear her muffled sobs through her hands. She smelled like a mixture of cigarette smoke, alcohol and something else that I couldn't identify.

"Mama?" I gingerly placed the palm of my hand on the small of her back feeling her quake beneath my fingers. "he doesn't deserve you, you're perfect, too perfect for that low life"
Without saying a word, she rested her head on my knee, I finally saw her eyes, red raw, cheeks tainted with tears and

black mascara that had smeared down her skin from crying, I wrapped her up in my arms like a blanket and rocked her gently back and forth like I was the mother and she was the child, like the mama and baby bear in my snow globe.

"Why can't I keep the men that I love?" She broke the silence, her voice sounding shaky and meek.

"I love you"

She didn't say it back but I knew she felt it, at least, I hoped she did.

"It's because of you brats" Suddenly her voice changed, became fuller, switching from sad to angry in a heartbeat "nobody wants to go out with someone with kids, you're the reason I can't keep a man"

She sat up so fast I was surprised she didn't give herself headrush. My mother was a beautiful woman, piercing blue eyes that could cut through you like a knife when she stared directly into yours, mousey brown hair that sat perfectly on her shoulders when it wasn't shoved carelessly into a bun at the back of her head, when she made an effort, she was easily the prettiest woman in any room.

"What have you got to say for yourself" She grabbed me by the fabric of my t-shirt and pulled me towards her, her long acrylic nails digging through my shirt to my skin "Huh? Say something!"

"Mama, please" I managed, placing both hands lightly on top of hers.

"You ruin everything!"

"Mama, you're scaring Alma and Cleo"

I motioned to my left, where Alma had emerged from the bedroom to see what was going on and Cleo sat curled around Alma's ankles. She let go of my shirt and I bounced back onto the couch, I could feel a trickle of blood leak from my chest, down my stomach and onto my trousers, she didn't mean it, she was just upset, she didn't mean it. She didn't say another word, just retreated to her room and slammed the door, I took Alma by the hand and grabbed Cleo and lead them back into the bedroom.

  Alma fell Asleep almost immediately that night, but Cleo sat on the floor playing with my old raggedy Anne doll that was more raggedy than Anne. I slipped my shirt off and stared at myself in the reflection of the window, all I could see was skin and bones, th shell of a person who was just trying to get through every day without falling apart. I could see the marks where her nails had been. Cleo watched as I used a tissue to wipe up the blood and slid on an old t-shirt that I had dug out of the washing. I couldn't sleep, my brain was too active, as I lay sandwiched between Alma and Cleo all I could think about was what my mother had said, had we ruined her life? Did she really think that or was it just said in the heat of the moment? On that note I felt myself sitting up, carefully as to not wake my sisters up and my feet walked me to the door, slipped my shoes on and carried me out of the house and down the street, whenever I was angry or upset I'd make my way to the park that sat on the corner of out street, sit on a swing and count the stars in the sky. it was dark and the light from the street lamps barely lit up the path in front of me, that's when I saw her, the same girl Alma and I had saw that morning in the same place we had seen her, sitting at the edge of the garden, I caught her eye and she offered me a welcome yet timid smile, it was the first time I had seen any kind of emotion on her face, I took a detour from where I was planning to go and I proceeded down the road towards her residence, it was as if I no longer has control over my legs and where they took my body and before I knew it, I was standing at the iron gates of the house at the end of the street, the house no one went near because they were convinced it was spooky and haunted, the house that was faintly lit like that of one in a horror film. It was bigger than any other house in the street, it appeared menacing and imposing, looming over its over grown garden with gnarled branches and grass reaching for the sky, casting a dark shadow that seemed to stretch on forever, the windows looked like empty eye sockets, no signs of any kind of life within them, the only light from them being that of the light from the moon, the house seemed to hang to one side, the roof was weathered and the paint on the wooden panels was peeling off, it was as if the house was alive and sad and afraid. My legs were shaking and my palms sweating but still I stood frozen to the spot.

"Wynter... My name, it's Wynter" I stumbled over my words as my tongue was stuck to the roof of my mouth. "What's your name?"
Silence, the girl bowed her head, I hadn't noticed before but her dress was torn and filth ridden and she was so bony that if she turned sideways she'd disappear completely, her dress hung loosely to her skin like it was at least 3 sizes too big. I wondered if that was what people saw when I walked into a room. I sat myself down on the pavement across from her, her eyes darted from one side to the other in frantic fear, they were green, like a cat my neighbour once had before it was hit by a car, she turned her face towards me, the light from the streetlights illuminating her features, her hair was jet black and was so long I was sure she could probably sit on it if she really wanted to, it looked like it had never been brushed and stuck up on the top of her scalp, dancing in the light breeze, she was pale, like a ghost and had a cluster of freckles that occupied each rosy cheek.

"Do you speak English? Because I know a little bit of French, well, I can say hello and goodbye and that I like to swim but that's about it" The silence continued "Can you speak at all?"

Remember when I said sometimes talking to Cleo was like talking to a brick wall? I was wrong, this was like talking to a brick wall. The girl stared right though me, as if she had never seen another human before, her eyes focused on mine, at one point I thought she was trying to move me with her mind.

"Aren't you cold?"

She was shivering like a leaf and her teeth were chittering so it was obvious she was, we were in the middle of winter and she was dressed in short sleeved pale blue dress made of the thinnest material I had ever seen. her legs were bare and she wasn't wearing any shoes, she was like a creature not of this world. At first she shook her head then eventually switched to a nod, I slipped my jumper off and slithered it through the bars on the gate, she held it in her hands for a moment, her fingers running over the soft material before putting it on. The corners of her mouth crept up to an almost smile, it was the first hint of happiness that I had seen from her since we had met but as quickly as it came, it disappeared.

    I sat with the girl with no name for at least another hour, I told her about my mother, how she would most likely drink herself into an early grave, I told her about how one day I was going to get out of this town and travel Europe in a camper van how I didn't want to get married because I didn't want to have to take care of a man child but how I did want children so I'd probably adopt and she listened, I knew she was listening because she never averted her eyes from my own and every now and then she'd nod involuntarily... I barely knew her, in fact I didn't know her at all, but for some strange reason I deemed her trustworthy enough to tell all my deepest secrets to, I was pouring my heart out to a complete stranger, probably because she was the first person who I had met who may understand me. Our moment was cut short by what sounded like the slamming of a door, without missing a beat the girl turned her head so quick I was surprised it didn't turn all the way around on her neck, suddenly, she scrambled to her feet in a blind panic and turned her head back to where I was.

"Wait!" I rose to my feet to meet her glance "I don't even know your name…"

"Violet" She whispered so quiet it faded in with the wind.

"What?"

"My name is Violet"

Before I knew it she had disappeared through the blades of overgrown grass and into the shadows, I waited for a moment to see if she would re-emerge but she didn't so I turned around and made my way back home, unable to get her off my mind, I had so many questions, who was she? Why was she outside in the dark of night? Where were her shoes? As I lay on the mattress that night crammed between Cleo and Alma she's all I thought about.

VIOLET

  I've always been afraid of the dark, ever since I can remember, I think it's because you never know what might come out of it, monsters, demons, your worst fears, but I knew it was going to be alright, I had my nightlight that my father bought me, it was a purple pearl inside a white clam and the pearl was the light, it wasn't very bright but it kept the monsters away, most of them anyway. At night time though, I would go outside, I wasn't supposed to, but I did it anyway, I liked the way that the cold air felt on my face and how the grass brushed against my skin, like it was just me and the earth, that's where I met her for the first time. She said her name was Wynter, which I thought was odd because that was a season, not a name, I had seen her walk past many times, with another girl, she always seemed rushed, like she had to be somewhere quickly and I always wondered where. I was minding my own business when she approached me.
  "Wynter... My name, it's Wynter" She was wearing a yellow night dress that had seen better days, with a jumper pulled over the top and worn in white trainers, she seemed a tad frightened, I was too "What's your name?"
I rarely saw children my own age, and when I did see them, I did not talk to them.
  "Are you cold?"
I was cold, so cold my skin felt like it was burning, I nodded so she passed me her jumper through the fence, why? I had no idea, but I took it and wrapped it around myself, feeling the soft material against me, like a warm hug. She told me about her life, unprompted, though it did peak my interest, it seemed hard but Wynter still seemed happy, like it didn't phase her.

"My sisters are great though, I have two sisters, Alma and Cleo... Alma is 5 and Cleo is 1, thy can be a handful but I still love them..."
I never had any sisters or brothers, no one to tell secrets to at night when we should have been in bed sleeping, no one to fight with then laugh it off, someone to sneak midnight snacks with. I lived with my adoptive father, he took me in at age three as my mother and father decided they didn't want me. I didn't remember them at all, not one bit, I often wondered what they were doing, did they ever think about me? Did they have any regrets? Were they happy? My father was a strict man, a scary man, most of the time it was his way or no way at all, when he was on one of his rage fuelled episodes it was best to stay out of his way, it was one of those nights.

"I don't have too many friends, actually, I kinda keep myself to myself, but maybe we could be friends..." Wynter continued.
I actually didn't have any friends either, I spent most of my days at home, staring at the walls, I never went to school, my father told me it was to protect me, but from what? What out there was scarier than in my own home? I had always wanted to go to a real school, to learn about English and Science and art, to go out with friends, things I only knew about through TV, Wynter didn't realise how lucky she was.

Wynter was a pretty girl, her hair was chestnut brown with some natural lighter highlights as if she had been out in the sun, it appeared to come down past her shoulders but was shoved messily into a ponytail and was wavy like the ocean. Her eyes were emerald green and round like the buttons on her night dress and she had an equal cluster of freckles on each cheek like they had been placed there intentionally on top of her creamy coloured skin but something I did notice about Wynter was she seemed slightly tired with purple bags resting beneath her heavy eyes, she appeared to carry the whole entire world on her shoulders. I suddenly realised that I was in a daze, that I hadn't been listening but Wynter just kept on talking, oblivious. All of a sudden I was brought back to earth by the sharp sound of a slamming door, crap, it was my father, he had noticed I was gone, I was dead. I could feel my heart pounding in my chest, it felt like it was about to jump out.

"Violet..." I told her.

"What?" Wynter queried, a puzzled look on her face.

"My name is Violet..."

I rose abruptly to my feet and bolted towards the house, I could see him through the window, his silhouette pacing back and forth, I couldn't tell if he was worried, angry or both. I took a deep breath before opening the door and stepping inside.

"Violet?!?"

I was stopped in my tracks as my father marched over and towered over me, angry, he was definitely angry.

"I... I... I'm really sorry..."

"Do you know why we have rules, Violet..."

"So I can be safe...."

"Correct, you don't know what it's like out there, I do, how can I protect you if you don't listen to me?

"I'm sorry, I just thought..."

"You don't want to spend the night in the confinement do you?"

I shook my head persistently, I did not want that. The confinement was a hole in the ground underneath the house, that you entered through a trap door on the basement ground that was hidden beneath a rug. There were no lights in the Confinement, it was small, damp, cold and dark and you had to climb down a ladder to get to it, my father often threatened it at a punishment but he had only carried it out a handful of times but those times were enough for me to never want to go down there again, the door locked from the outside so there was no way of me getting out, I could be in there for up to a week, my father only coming down to feed me once a day if he even remembered. My father walked me downstairs to the basement, the door shrieking piercingly as he pushed it open, where I would sleep on a thin mattress on a camp bed that was so slim I was more or less sleeping on the cold hard ground. There was no heating in my basement bedroom and the only thing I had to keep me warm was a babies blanket that barely covered my legs. The walls were built with brick and stone and other than my camp bed, there was no other furniture down there.

"I'll come check on you later…"

I climbed beneath the thin blanket that I had had for as long as I could remember, curling myself into a ball because it was the only way I could keep warm and drifted into a light sleep, I could never fall fully asleep, I never knew when I needed to be alert.

I knew whenever my father entered my room, I could feel his eyes on me like a hawk. I pretended to be a sleep so that he would just leave, I felt the back of his hand on my cheek, stroking it softly, his face so close to me I could feel his warm breath, it smelled like a mixture of mint and cigarette smoke. He waited for a moment before standing up, I could hear the sound of him walking away, I kept my eyes closed until I heard the door to the basement shut. My father left every single day to go to work, he served in the army for 10 years but now he worked as a caretaker, he could be out some days from the break of dawn until the dead of night and other days for just a few hours, I never knew which one it was going to be. I heaved my heavy bones up out of bed, pressing my bare feet onto the cold concrete floor I stood up and headed up the stairs. I pressed my ear up against the door to see if my father was still at home, I heard nothing so I knew it was safe to come out.

When I emerged into the breezy outdoors, a familiar face was waiting for me, it was Wynter, what was she doing here? She was sitting with her legs crossed on the other side of the iron gate, she was reading, looking up from her book she spotted me and waved me over. I had no idea why she was here, but I was really happy that she was.

"Volet!"

I bounded over to the iron fence and sat down in front of her.

"I've been here for a while, I saw your dad leave for work, wasn't sure if you were gonna be coming out here today…" Wynter placed a folded over piece of paper into her book, closed it and stuffed it into her backpack. "I brought a game for us, do you like games?"

My father never played games with me, so I didn't know if I liked them, I shrugged timidly, Wynter offered me a warm smile before pulling a box out of her back pack.

"It's called operation, it's kinda weird, it's taking a bunch of bones out of this guy but if you buzz the sides, you lose and his nose goes red, my sisters love playing it, it's so fun…."

Wynter began setting up the game and I watched on in awe of her wild and free way of life, I wondered what it was like to feel and be so free. Wynter handed me what she explained was tweezers, I tentatively took them from her, not sure what to do.

"First, you take a card, then you pick out what the card says…" Wynter and I stared at one another for a moment before I averted my eyes and took a card from

the pile. "You got the wishbone, that's a tricky one!"
I looked to the strange board of a man with a red nose and many holes in his body and searched through the holes for the bone that matched the one on the card, I wondered if the bones inside my body looked like the bones inside his, once I had locked eyes with the correct one I slowly began to lower the tweezers into the hole, my hands were shaking but I was doing pretty well, I pinched the tweezers onto the wishbone and began to raise it up but my hand twitched and the man's nose went red and buzzed loudly causing me to jump.

"You'd make a terrible surgeon" Wynter laughed, her laugh smooth as honey, we were having fun, I hadn't had fun in a while.

WYNTER

In the weeks following my encounters with Violet, I saw her almost every day under the fall of darkness and early in the mornings, I got to know her father's schedule, when he would be there, when he wouldn't, I learned that on Mondays and Thursdays he left at 6AM, travel coffee cup in hand, on Saturdays and Sundays he worked nights, from 7PM until 7AM, he stayed at home Tuesdays and Fridays so those were the days I avoided, I'd slip myself out from between Cleo and Alma, past my mother who would be passed out on the couch and I'd head out of the door and sneak down the street to her house where she would always be waiting, her eyes lighting up upon my approach. I'd talk and she would listen, in fact, since she had told me her name, she hadn't uttered two words to me, I was beginning to wonder if she was a mute or if she was just painfully shy, the most I could ever get out of her was a nod or a shake of the head when I asked her a question.

"Are you hungry?" I asked her, she thought for a moment before gently nodding her head. I reached into my backpack and pulled out a ham sandwich I had packed in case I got hungry, tore it apart and handed half to Violet, cautiously, she took it in her grasp like it was diseased, between two fingers. "Don't worry, I promise it isn't poisoned" I joked but she didn't laugh but simply sat for a moment staring at the sandwich intently. "Violet, you can eat it, it's okay." Violet brought the sandwich to her lips uncertainly and took the smallest bite I had ever seen before smiling to herself and demolishing the rest in seconds, she was an enigma, a paradox, the only thing I knew about her was that she lived with her dad and she now, evidently, liked ham sandwiches.

"You should come over to my house some time,

meet my sisters, you'd really love them, they're the best kind of crazy"

Violet's eyes widened like I had just told her that her puppy had died and she reached her hand through the bars of the gate that separated us and placed it on my knee like she was trying to comfort me though I didn't need to be comforted, her hands were caked in mud and ice cold but still I placed a hand on top of hers because I knew she needed it more than I did.

"I've never had a silent friend before" I laughed, Violet took her hand back through the bars in a hurry and gasped, her wide eyes softening.

"Friends?" She relaxed, though I couldn't get past the part where she had just spoken to me.

"Yes, friends"

My mother had barely left her bed in weeks other than to move to the couch to do similar to what she had been doing in bed, moping, she'd also leave to use the toilet and occasionally to grab a snack from the kitchen but mostly she stayed in bed, when I wasn't in school I was her attendant, I made her cups of coffee, changed the water in her hot water bottle and made sure she was eating enough, I was the mother that I had never had. I had never seen her so depressed; my mother could be up and down a lot but this seemed, different. I sat myself down beside her on the bed where she lay curled up, cocooned under her duvet, I would have thought she was dead if I couldn't hear the breath in her lungs gasping for air like she was drowning in her own despair. I could hear Alma and Cleo playing in the Livingroom and I wished I was with them, being childlike, playing with dolls, using my imagination but I had responsibilities, so I couldn't. I thought about Violet, what her life was like, if it was a life I'd have liked to swap with, if she was able to be carefree or if she was confined to her own obligations, I wouldn't know, because Violet knew so much about me, yet I knew so little about her,

"Wynter, can you grab me a glass of water from the kitchen?"
I slid myself down from the bed and made my way into the kitchen, passing Alma and Cleo who were rolling a ball back and forth on the floor, there were no clean glasses so I rinsed one that was sitting on the worktop and filled it to the brim with water and took it back to my mother, I helped her to sit up and held the glass to her lips, she sipped it slowly.

"Mama" I trailed off biting my lip, I had her full attention for the first time in as long as I could remember and I didn't know what to do with it.

"What is it Wynter?"

"there's this girl, she lives down the street, she's really shy and I can't seem to get her to talk to me all that much and I don't know what more I can do, I really want to be her friend"
My mother took one final sip of water before pushing it away with her hand I sat it on her bedside cabinet.

"well, she might just need time Wynie, maybe she's just shy…"

"I gave her time, I dunno if she's just really reserved or just plain weird"
I hadn't spoken to my mother like this in as long as I could remember and I wasn't sure how long this version of my mother would last so I was trying to savour and cherish every single moment before normality was restored.

"well, there's nothing wrong with being a little weird."
She was right, all the best people were a little weird, heck I was a little weird, I just had to find a way to get through to Violet, to show her that she could trust me like I trusted her.

"When I was seven years old, I peed myself in front of my whole class." Violet looked up from whatever she was doing, perplexed. "I've never been on a plane... I am so terrified of public speaking I'd rather stick pins in my eyes than do it, see, weird, you don't need to be embarrassed by any skeletons you have in your closet because everyone has weird little quirks, you can trust me Violet, I promise" I sat myself down on the pavement I usually sat at when I came to see Violet, still she remained mute. "Violet, it's getting old now, I know you can speak, so speak..." The radio silence continued "This is hopeless, okay, you win, I'm not doing it anymore"
I rose to my feet and began to walk away, I didn't have the energy to fight with her or force her to speak.

"Wait...Wynter" It was quiet, but it was Violet, I turned back around to face her, she had tears in her eyes, waiting to fall down her cheeks. "most of the time I can't find the right words to say and sometimes I use the wrong ones and I get muddled up, so I just stay quiet to stop that from happening, I don't want people to think I'm dumb..."
There it was, trust, for once my mother was right, these things take time. I sat back down, I didn't know where to go next, I didn't have a plan but Violet was talking so it felt like a win to me.

"I can help you if you like?"
I saw a smile slowly creep onto her face until she was beaming like I had just told her she was going to Disney World but in reality I had only offered my assistance and she seemed to appreciate that, that was enough for her.

Over the following weeks I began meeting Violet everyday afterschool, until her father came home and she had to run off to greet him and then later on at night after my sisters were asleep, I'd sit and do my homework and she would make daisy chains. I'd split a sandwich with her and we'd just talk about nothing, it was as if we had known each other all of our lives. .

"Math should be banned, when am I ever gonna need to know the square route of X? Or the names for the different types of triangles? Never, that's when…"
Violet looked up from her creation, puzzled.

"You're not one of those people who like math are you? I mean I enjoy school but math is just a cruel and unusual punishment, what school do you go to anyways, I've not seen you around, do you go to one of those fancy pants private schools?"

"School?"

"Yeah, you *do* go to school don't you?"
Violet bit down on her lip hard and tucked a strand of her fine hair behind her ear before grabbing my gaze with her piercing yet fear-filled eyes, timidly she shook her head.

"So, are you home schooled?"

"My father says schools are just government run institutions that mould and manipulate the minds of young people and that's a sin."

"I mean, he's not wrong, they are basically a prison." I paused, taking my English literature book from my book bag. "English lit is my favourite subject, here, To Kill a Mockingbird, it's one of my favourites" I handed her the book, she stared at the front cover for a moment a blank expression on her face. "You can borrow it if you like, I've read it 3 times."
Violet reached her hand through the bars and grasped the book, for a moment she stared down at it, almost mesmerised before her expression dropped and she pushed it back through to me.

"What? You don't like reading?"

"I…" Violet bit down hard on her lip again and began playing with her hands uncomfortably. "I can't read"

"Oh" I filed the book back into my book bag.

"Well, there's a girl in my class who has dyslexia, it's nothing to be embarrassed about, she's come a long way since they got a teaching assistant to help her... I could help you Violet! I'm a straight A student, it will be fun, would you like that?"
She stared at me bewildered, her eyes wide, like a deer in headlights. I reached through the bars, like she was a prisoner in her own jail and took hold of her hand, gently squeezing it, in a way to comfort her, she softened to a smile.

"I'd really like that..."

I spent the following weeks teaching Violet, we would read books together and she'd write letters over and over and over again until she was happy with how they looked, I'd give her homework to do, words to learn and sentences to write, I never did ask her why she struggled, but I wanted to help her, I knew what it was like to feel alone, I knew what it was like to feel like no one cared, so I wanted Violet to know that someone cared about her, that I cared about her.

"What's that word?"

"It's Pterodactyl, a type of dinosaur"

"Why is there a P at the beginning of Pterodactyl?"

"I never understood that either... The English language is weird" Violet nodded her head whilst flipping through the textbook that I had "borrowed" from school. "So, is it dyslexia you have or some other thing?" I handed her a spelling book that belonged to my sister.

"What's that?"

"I guess not then, so are you home-schooled"
She stared at me with a blank expression on her face, as if I had two heads, like she hadn't the slightest clue what I was talking about. "Who teaches you?"

"ummm... My father does, he's a really good

teacher, I just don't listen, that's why I'm behind"
Something I had noticed about Violet was that she was always on edge, she was always fidgeting, always jumpy like she was afraid of something, maybe she was just devoid of social interaction but I just brushed it off, she was my friend and I didn't have many of those.

    That night, when I was sneaking back into my house, Alma awakened with a groan, she snuggled into me as I carefully slipped in between her and Cleo.
    "Wynnie. Where do you go every night?"
I hadn't noticed that she would miss me when I creeped out the bedroom at 11PM every night.
    "I go to see my friend"
I laid my head against the folded up sweatshirt that acted as my pillow and pulled Alma into me.
    "At night?"
    "She's rarely out during the day"
    "Why not?"
I didn't know why not, I didn't ask why not but it was a question that played on my mind, why mostly night time? Was she allergic to sunlight? I pondered my thoughts as I drifted off to sleep though even in my deepest dreams, I didn't know the answers.

    When I was 5 years old I would spend most weekend at Genevieve's house, she lived across the road and she had everything a little girl could ever want, everything that I never had, a functional family, a tidy house, a trampoline and all the toys a child could possibly want, so every Saturday morning whilst my mother slept, I'd leave through the back door and sneak around the house, run across the road and ring the doorbell of the Paxton's house, her mother, Laura, would always answer and greet me with the warmest embrace, there were many times during my childhood where I wished Laura was my own mother, she'd usher me inside where Genevieve would either be practicing her piano or working on her ballet in the dance studio that they had inside their house, I'd wait for her to finish and then we'd play in her back garden that was literally the size of my entire house, if not bigger and we'd play for hours. Over the years things had changed but whenever I needed someone to be blunt and brutally honest I'd go to Genevieve, our relationship was an odd one, it was built on a foundation of making fun of one another and us not speaking for weeks but still being there for one another when we needed it. I was there for her when her Granma passed away and she was there for me the night my mother almost OD'd.

"Wynter, oh it's so good to see you!" Laura had opened the door before I even had the chance to ring the doorbell and had scooped me up into her arms, Laura was the epitome of joy, always smiling, always laughing, her hair was midnight black and constantly styled immaculately in waves like the ones in the ocean, her crescent shaped eyebrows bordered her strong brown eyes and her voice was sweet like sugar. Her lips, dawning shiny pink lip gloss, broke into a smile that sent electricity though my body and put me at ease. "Come on in, Genevieve is just finishing off her breakfast."
Laura lead me down the lengthy hallway which appeared to be a shrine to Genevieve with childhood pictured, awards and trophies, and artwork, if Genevieve had touched it, I was sure it was on that wall. The hall led straight to the kitchen where Genevie was sitting at the breakfast bar, spooning cereal into her mouth. She turned her head to me so I knew she had noticed me but she didn't acknowledge my existence and went straight back to reading whatever she was reading.

"G, Wynter's here" Laura nudged me in the back to step forward before leaving us alone in the kitchen, I scrambled up onto the bar stool next to Genevieve.

"I just thought it might be nice if we hung out, y'know, for old times' sake?"

Genevieve liked to pretend she didn't have feelings but I could see a smile trying not to sneak its way onto her face, she slammed her book down onto the counter and swivelled towards me.

"ooh fun." She said sarcastically hopping down off the chair, she began walking towards the French doors that lead out to the garden. "Well, are you coming or not?"

When Genevieve said jump, you were supposed to say how high so I followed her lead out into the garden.

"do you remember when we were like 8 and we decided we were going to run away, go to France and live under the Eiffel tower?" I spoke throwing myself down onto the freshly cut grass

She smirked to herself thoughtfully.

"Yeah" She laughed "we were going to buy a campervan between us"

"A pink and purple one"

"…And I was going to marry a Frenchman and you were going to start your business, what was it again?"

"A…"

"Hat maker…" We said simultaneously before beginning to hoot with laughter, Genevieve's guarded posture diminished and she sat down on the grass next to me, for a moment neither of us said a word.

"What were you running from?" I queried.

"What?"

"Well, I know what I was running from, what were you running from?"

Genevieve bit her lip and looked down, something in her eyes suddenly seemed broken.

"Nothing, my life is perfect"

Nobody's life is perfect and I knew this more than anyone, you could have everything in the world and still be unhappy, we spent the rest of the afternoon gossiping about our classmates and not talking about the elephant in the room.

"why don't we hang out so much anymore?"

"We're just different people Wynter, it's not that deep..."

"but we used to be so close..."

I watched as Genevieve pondered her thoughts and I knew that she was thinking about the memories, because she smiled to me fondly, she didn't often show her feelings, most of the time she was cold, calculated and detached, but that day I saw a more human side of Genevieve.

"I better go, my sisters will be wondering where I am" I rose to my feet, rubbing the grass from my trousers.

"Oh, Wynter, before you go..."

"Yeah?"

"I have some science homework... Would you mind?"

I sighed as Genevieve reached into her bag and pulled out a folder, I took it from her, just when I thought I was in, she proved to me that I would never truly be in all the way, I wasn't popular but I wasn't unpopular, I was just, there.

"Thanks, I'll have it done for Monday..."

"Wynter you're a gem".

Monday rolled around far too quickly and suddenly I found myself back in the hallways of Sherwood's' youth detention centre, otherwise known as school. It always felt like a cross between a prison and a zoo, kids jumping all over the place like monkeys, but teachers laying down the arm of the law like guards, it was a strange dynamic. On Mondays first thing I had art class with Miss Giles, in the

Bees Beckett Memorial room that was dedicated to a former student of the school. Miss Giles was one of those people who just radiated kindness, her voice was quiet and her demeanour unassuming, she was stunning to look at which was why I was so surprised that she wasn't married. My class filtered in like caged animals at feeding time and we all grabbed an easel, a palette that had been set up with paints in all different colours and paint brushes that Miss Giles pointed out were at the front of the class beside the bookshelf. I had never been the most artistic of people, I was book smart, not creative. Genevieve took the easel next to myself and Orla took the one on my other side.

"You got the homework?"
As usual I handed her the folder like we were doing a low-profile drug deal and she slipped it into her bag.

"But would it hurt you to do your own homework?" Genevieve slipped me the coins away from the naked eye and I placed them into my pocket.

"Actually, it would, the thought of doing it gave me heart palpitations, oh, be still my beating heart" Genevieve said mockingly and Orla let out a small giggle. "Come on Wynter, have a sense of humour." She nudged me with her pointed knifelike elbows and before I could stop it I could feel a smile on route to my face.

"With mother's day coming up, I thought we could do something for our mothers, anything you want, anything at all" Miss Giles spoke, waving a paintbrush around enthusiastically, she was always this animated, like a character from one of the cartoon shows that I occasionally put on for my sisters when our electricity was in working order.

"What are you going to do?"
"What do you mean?"
"Well, you're mother isn't exactly, y'know..."

"What's that supposed to mean?"

"Wynter, we both know she spends most days drunk and sleeping on the couch, that is when she isn't hooking up with every guy in town..."

Although I knew she was right, I could feel the anger bubbling up inside of me and all I could see was red and before I could stop myself I had kicked the leg of the easel causing it to tumble onto Orla, who was oblivious to life which in turn made her fall over, it seemed to all happen in slow motion, like a car crash, I knew it was happening but I just couldn't stop it.

"Wynter Jones, see me after class".

I watched as all of my classmates got to leave, whilst I, still burning in my brain with thoughts of what Genevieve had said sat at a desk at the front of the class where you were placed if you misbehaved, I had never been in trouble in my entire life, I always completed my homework on time, never talked back and got good grades but somehow I found myself lumped with the delinquents of the school, Chase Eastwood, was constantly in detention for firing spit balls at the teacher, Rose Myers, most known for purposefully flooding the girls bathroom so that we'd all be sent home, Jamie Goodwin, kicked a ball through the school window when the office staff told him that it would be confiscated, and now Wynter Jones, injured a fellow student.

"Wynter, what's going on, this is so not like you" Miss Giles sat herself down on the desk at the front of the class and turned her full attention to me. I couldn't look her in the eyes because she'd know something was wrong so I stared out the window and counted the lilies in the garden that had been planted by the third grade as a nature project, if I ignore my problems they'll go away, right? "Wynter, talk to me."

I hated when adults pushed kids to talk, I had nothing to

talk about, my life was great, a little unconventional but still great. Miss Giles sighed and pushed herself up from the desk, now standing over me like a tree. "What did Genevieve Paxton say to you to make you so upset" The woman had eyes like a hawk, one lily, two lily, three lily, four lily. "Wynter..."
"It's this whole mothers day thing"
"What do you mean?"
Before I could stop myself, it came out, like vomit, spurting from inside the pit of my stomach.
"My mother is dead"
Why did I say that? Why did I say that? The guilt immediately began to eat me up inside.
"Oh Wynter, I'm so sorry I didn't know" I'm the worst person in the world, I thought to myself as Miss Giles face changed from frustration to pure pity and she threw her arms around me pulling me into a hug that I really didn't deserve. "Well, you just paint whatever you want, or you can help me with a few things, whatever you want to do."
I bowed my head in shame as Miss Giles held me.

On the walk home from school with Alma clutching my hand I saw Violet sitting in the usual place, staring out onto the street, she noticed me and I waved, but something startled her and she jolted her head almost 180 degrees towards the house and before I knew it, she was gone.
"Why does she always sit there like that Wynter?"
"I'm really not sure...."
We walked on in silence and I ran every possible scenario over in my head, Violet was strange, her mannerism, her nervous disposition, everything about her made me wonder what was going on in her life, but I didn't know her like that yet, I needed her to trust me more, I was going to get her to trust me more.

VIOLET

A... Is for apple, a piece of fruit I had seen many times in the kitchen but had never eaten. B... Is for books, a new-found love of mine, thanks to Wynter. C.... Is for cake, the thing you're supposed to get on your birthday but I had never even had a birthday party. D... Is for dog, like the terrifying creature that lived across the road, brown in colour, constantly growling. I was doing well with my reading, Wynter had taught me and I was so grateful for that, every night in my dimly lit basement room I read through the spelling book that she had gifted me and learned to spell a new word by scrawling it with a stone onto the wall. Today's word, E... Is for elephant, the hardest word I had done so far, the picture was of a beautiful creature I had never seen before. I sat down on the freezing stony floor and next to my previous word began writing the word on the wall. Suddenly the door to the basement swung open and my father emerged at the top of the stairs, quickly I shoved the book beneath my camp bed.

"Violet! I've got a job for you..." I stood up abruptly and remained glued to the floor for a moment. "Well, what are you waiting for?"
Hastily I stood to attention before joining my father up the stairs, most of the times the jobs were cleaning the toilet, mopping the kitchen or sweeping his study, but not today. I followed him to the door and then outside, strange, my father never encouraged me to step into the outside world, I bit down on my lip nervously. We approached the shed at the back corner of the garden, it was creepy, falling apart and needed a good paint job. He opened the door, cobwebs hanging from every single inch of the wall.

"Alright, in you go..." I stepped into the shed.
"This is for disobeying me yesterday, maybe you'll learn to

obey the rules by polishing off my guns and know that if you pull a stunt like that again, going to confinement will be the least of your worries." My father raised his eyebrows and nodded towards a specific gun that hung on the wall, the biggest one, I knew what he meant, he then tossed me an old rag and slammed the door, I heard the bolt lock fasten and I was left in almost complete darkness.

    I had very few memories from my very early years, just bits and pieces, I remembered a large garden with purple and pink flowers at the front and a little fence that was painted blue, I remembered a song about sunshine, "you are my sunshine my only sunshine...." And I remembered the sound of the voice that sung it and I remembered a young girl, her image so clear in my head, she was older than me, blonde poker straight hair, pink glasses over hazel eyes but other than those few memories, everything else was black and bleak. I was grateful to my father for adopting me, sure he was harsh and sometimes mean, but I'd rather that than being somewhere I wasn't wanted. I polished each gun with care reciting my letters aloud. A is for apple, B is for book, C is for cake, D is for dog, E is for elephant... A is for apple, B is for book, C is for cake, D is for dog, E is for elephant... There were 12 guns in total.

    I wasn't sure how long I was in the shed but it was as long as my father took to go to and come home from work, it had become icy cold and I was using an old tarp that I had found to keep myself warm. The door opened slowly; my father offered me a smile.

    "have you learned your lesson, Violet?" I nodded placing the tarp back where I had found it. "I don't like punishing you Violet, you know that, come on..."
He turned around crouching down, waiting for me to jump

onto his back, hesitantly, I did and he walked me into the house, I knew where we were heading, my father's room, my heart sunk, we entered the room and he shut the door behind us.

  The following day, once my father had left for work, I took my usual place by the fence. Everything felt numb, I pulled some daisies from the ground and I wondered if they felt pain when I did that, did they feel anything at all? I remained there all day, even seeing Wynter and her sister, my heart suddenly felt full. I made eye contact with her, I smiled and she waved.

  "VIOLET!!!" I heard my name echo through the air. I hadn't even seen or heard him come home, I was in for it now. I ran inside, my father nowhere to be seen, the door to my basement room was open and I knew that's where he was. I crept slowly down the stairs, he was facing the other way but he turned to face me, he was holding my spelling book.

  "What's this, Violet?"

  "It's a spelling book, I found it, must have fallen out of someone's backpack..." I lied.

  "So, you stole it...?"

  "No, I... I..."

  "Do I not teach you enough? You ungrateful little twerp!"

My father tore the book clean down the middle, placed the halves in front of one another and tore it again, it felt like he had taken my heart and tore it too.

  "No..." I fell hard to my knees, tears filling up in my eyes.

  "That's it, little girls who don't listen have to be punished."

My father headed to the back of the basement, lifted the rug that sat over a little trap door, pulling the handle it opened. He grabbed my wrist and yanked me to my feet with so much force he lifted my feet off the ground. That trap door, lead to the confinement. My father dragged me kicking and screaming over to the hole, grazing my knees on the concrete and lowered me into the hole slamming the door behind me, I climbed the ladders and began banging on the door but it was no use, I wasn't getting out of there. The room was almost completely black except a tiny barred window at the top near the door. I laid myself down on the on the floor, it was freezing cold, I drifted off to sleep.

WYNTER

In the weeks following my odd encounter with Violet, I didn't see her much at all, it was as if she had vanished, I looked for her walking to school she wasn't there, on the way back from school the garden was empty, even after night had fallen she was nowhere to be seen. I was beginning to think that I had dreamt her up, that she wasn't real at all, that she was just a figment of my imagination, I did have quite an elaborate mind.

"Wynter I'm hungry" Alma moaned as she trailed by my side scuffing her feet, I didn't often bring her with me on my weekly trip to the convenience store, only when I had to but Caroline had called me that morning and said she had come down with something and couldn't take Cleo so both Alma and I had taken the day off school.

"you just had breakfast"

"Only a banana"

That was the only food that we had in the house that hadn't gone off and even they were nearing the end of their lives. We stepped over the threshold of the doorway greeted by a soft smile from Polly, her daughter, Ava sitting at her feet playing with two toy cars, ramming them into one another and making exploding sounds, she looked up to us and cowered behind her mother's legs.

"No school today Wynter?"

I was hoping that she wouldn't notice but hoping only ever got you so far.

"Cleo's a bit under the weather and mamas worried we'll catch it so she kept us all home." I lied

"But she still sent you to the store?"

Crap, caught out, I shuffled uncomfortably on the spot, Cleo becoming increasingly heavy on my hip.

"yeah um, we're kind of running low on

supplies…"

Polly looked sceptical but nodded nonetheless and passed me the usual groceries, plus an apple to stop Alma from moaning. I handed Cleo off to Alma to put the change in my pocket.

"How old is she?"

"She's one"

"I remember when my little Miss was that small, they're the best at that age"

She clearly didn't know the little demon that was Cleo Jones.

"Yeah, she is something"

"Now my little baby is about to turn 4, not so little anymore"

Ava was tall for her age, she looked at least 6 or 7, with caramel coloured skin and dark brown almost black hair, she looked absolutely nothing like her mother, if I didn't know any better I'd have sworn she was adopted.

"I don't see your mother around here that often anymore Wynter, how is she doing?"

Great, more questions.

"Yeah, she's fine, just busy with work and stuff"

Another lie, but it kept Polly at arm's length and it kept my sanity in order, though I was worried that one day my lies would catch up to me. Granma Jones always said "a lie is a lie, a white lie is a lie, a half-truth is a lie, a hidden truth is a lie, a lie is a lie." Oh, how disappointed she would be if she knew.

"Ahhh yes, I can relate, this store doesn't run itself"

I eventually managed to escape the nosiest person in town and we began on our journey home though it felt like the longest walk ever with Alma complaining "My feet hurt", "are we almost home?", "I'm hungry again" and reminding me again, why I rarely took her places. Through all of the chaos though, I was stopped in my tracks causing Alma to skid in her already worn trainers on the pavement.

"What is it Wynter?"

We were standing outside the house at the end of the street where Violet resided, I gulped hard, it was like a house from one of those scary movies my mother liked to watch, you could almost sense the thunder and lightning surrounding it, I was intrigued my brain processing at a hundred miles per hour, I had only ever been as far as the outside of the gate, should I? Shouldn't I? I should, I handed Cleo to Alma and instructed her not to move from that spot, she seemed perplexed but before she could ask me any questions I had made a bee line for the gate, I wondered if I was small enough to slip through the bars, I wasn't, I needed another way in, I needed to stop my brain from spinning at a hundred miles per hour, wondering if Violet even existed or if I had just made her up, I needed to know that I wasn't crazy, like my mother. There! Around the side there was a pathetic plastic style fence with pickets that could easily be bent out of shape, I had to try, I scurried around and began to pull at the pickets, it wasn't as easy as it looked but they did bend a little and I did manage to squeeze myself through but once on the other side I had to take a moment to get my strength back. The yard was huge much larger than any of the others in the street, it looked like it had been extended, that it hadn't always been so big, it was mainly covered in grass though most of the grass appeared to have died or hadn't been taken care of, I kept close to the building as I wandered further around the side so that I had less chance of being seen. What now? I hadn't thought this through, at the back corner of the yard there were some concrete stairs, I wondered where they led, for a moment I stayed frozen to the spot before I plucked up the courage to run to them, out in the open, hoping to not get caught. Most of the steps were broken and they wobbled when stepped on but still I made my way down to the lower part of the garden, it was eery down there, it felt wrong to even set foot on the soil, I began walking, scoping the place out, the ground crunching beneath my feet, when I rounded the corner and made my way down a further hilly grass bank, coming across what looked like a secret room, a cylinder of stone that was fully underground except the top that sat above ground with a singular window on its side, with bars on it, the voice inside my head was telling me to abandon ship. Before I could communicate with my brain to stop my feet from moving, they were walking towards this strange little extension of a building, crouching down and kneeling to look down into the window, there she was, her silhouette at least, why was she there? What had happened to her? Was she okay?

"Pst, Violet!" I whispered, she jumped with fright and approached the window, looking up towards me. She seemed shocked to see me but I was relieved to see her.

"Wynter, what are you doing here?" Violet queried, half whispering, half talking.

"I've been looking for you, I came to see you a couple of times but you weren't here, I got a little worried, also I had to know if you were okay, what is this place?"

"My father thought I stole that book you gave me, so he tore it and put me in here as punishment... I'm so sorry Wynter"

"It's okay Violet, we can just go tell him I gave it to you"

"No Wynter, he can't know you are here..."

"Why not?"

Violets eyes dropped to the floor; half of her face was in darkness but I could see that she had tears in her eyes.

"You can't be here Wynter" She didn't answer my

question.

"Why not?"

"I'm not allowed people over." She stuttered, avoiding eye contact.

"Your dad is that strict?"

Violet thought for a moment and then nodded her head.

"Well how about if you come over to mine?"

"like out of the yard?"

"Yeah, it'll be fun?"

"I don't think I can, he'd never allow it."

Violet struggled with her words, she thought carefully before each sentence like she didn't know how to string them together properly and she couldn't pronounce her s's, they came out in the sound "th".

"You mean your dad? Well, what if we don't tell him?"

"You mean sneak out? I don't know, what if I get caught?"

"What's the worst he could do, ground you? Confine you to your room?" Violet reached her small hand through the bars in the window, her wrists were so tiny I was afraid they'd just snap in half, I took her small frail hand in my own. "Besides, I'm your friend I won't get you into trouble, I promise."

Violet offered me a solemn smile like she'd never had a friend before, maybe she hadn't, maybe I was her first, she wrapped her fingers around my hand, it was the first time I had gotten the sense that she was fully comfortable in my company.

"Seriously Wynter you've got to go, be careful on the way out, don't get caught"

"See you tomorrow, by the gate?"

"I don't know how long I'll be in here for..."

"Violet, he's not gonna keep you in there for days, it's just a punishment..." Violet bit down on her lip,

something that I had noticed she did when she was nervous or thinking of her next move. "Tomorrow, by the gate?"
Violet nodded and I left her and headed back up the stairs, I waited until the coast was clear before making my way back to my sisters who were now sitting on the kerb using stones to draw shapes on the tar, Alma immediately jumped to her feet when she saw me coming, the look of angst written all over her face.

"Where did you go? I was so worried!" She flung her arms around my waist so tight that my breathing was almost restricted, it took all my might to prize her hands from my jumper, she was strong for such a tiny human.

"Just seeing my friend"

"The one you see at night time? What is her name? What does she look like? Can I play too?"
I took Alma by the hand and picked Cleo up onto my hip and we walked home. That night I could barely sleep, my brain was buzzing, even the sound of my mother in the next room with her newest man candy and whatever loud games they played at 3AM couldn't stop the buzz.

The next day I waited for Violet outside the gate of her house, it was early in the morning so the streets were empty, like a ghost town, haunted and eery, I had left Alma and Cleo at home in bed and snuck out of the house so that no one would hear me, though I was worried that Violet wouldn't come.

"Pst.... Wynter..."
She poked her head out from behind a cluster of bushes that lined the fence, I motioned to the area where I had entered the day before and she slipped herself through, she was abnormally thin and petite, what I'd expect from a child of 7 or 8, you could almost see the bones sticking through her skin whenever she moved, she was almost a

whole head smaller than me and I wasn't exactly a giant and still she wore no shoes.

"C'mon, let's go to the park" I prompted, leading the way, Violet trailing like a well-trained dog behind me. The park was only a stone's throw from where we were but Violet was limping so it took much longer.

"What happened to your leg?"

"My leg?"

"Your leg. You're limping."

"Stairs, I fell down them, I'm kind of clumsy" Violet blurted out, like she was just trying to get the words out of her brain.

"Sounds painful… And why do you never wear any shoes?"

Violet looked down at her feet, they were scorned, filthy and blistered but she didn't seem to mind too much, she focused her attention back to me shrugging her shoulders, I didn't ask her any more questions and we continued to walk in silence. Sherwood only had one park, it was small and outdated but still in the summer months many flocked to it for a shot on the home-made tyre swing or a climb on the climbing frame that was donated after the girl scouts raised funds from their bag packing in the local supermarket. Violet's face lit up like she had never seen a park before and immediately hobbled over to the tyre swing and jumped on, I ran to her side and began to push her back and forth as she giggled gleefully, her arms outstretched trying to catch the air, thump, that was short lived, Violet picked herself off of the ground, dusted herself off and began to beam, her smile almost reaching from one ear to the other, it was almost as if she couldn't feel pain, either that or she just didn't care.

"You know you need to hold on" I laughed "Or else you're gonna fall"

Violet didn't seem too worried about falling, she just

laughed it off. One thing I noticed about Violet in the short time that I had known her was that she had the attention span of my five-year-old sister Alma and an infantile like charm about her like she was unsure of the world around her and unsure of herself, she wanted to soak up every piece of information possible, it was peculiar but still endearing. She ran to the climbing frame and clumsily began to scale it wobbling, like a baby deer learning how to walk, eventually reaching the top, from there she stood looking around like it had been the first time she had been out of the confines of her own garden, maybe it was her first time out, her father seemed like he ran a pretty tight ship so it wouldn't be all too shocking if he didn't let her out, he was probably protective, after all, Violet was incredibly fragile.

"Everything is so small from up here"

"That's just perspective"

I climbed up and sat next to her.

"Perspective?"

"yeah, it's like the way we see things, when we're close, we see them really big and when we are further away, they're smaller."

"Perspective..." She repeated, smiling.

Violet closed her eyes and tipped her head back, a cold gentle breeze cut me deep into my core but she seemed immune to the plummeting temperature, she was made of steel, invincible, maybe she was really a superhero, maybe she was just, different, good different but still different. As I gazed over towards where she had now lay down, I wondered what went on inside her head, what her thought process was, whether she just saw the beauty in everything that caught her eye, or if this really was the first time she was seeing it.

"Maybe some time you can come over to mine, meet my sisters"

Violet gently nodded her head, so gently I barely even noticed.

"I used to have a sister…"

Violet opened her eyes and rose to the seating position, suddenly uncomfortable.

"What do you mean used to?"

Abruptly she jumped down from the wooden climbing frame, landing on the concrete below, for a moment she remained silent.

"I'm not sure" She froze to the spot, like someone had glued her feet to the ground. "Can you walk me home?"

As she had asked, I walked her home, suddenly she had gone from curious about the world to wanting to hide from it. She walked quickly, at least two steps ahead of me, like she was in a hurry, like she was against the clock, like she was afraid of something and as I watched her climb through the gap in the fence, she didn't turn back.

PEYTON

When winter Jones didn't show up to school for a couple of days I did worry. Wynter was my most intelligent student, genius level intelligence but she often seemed like she carried a heavy load. I wasn't sure what her home life was like but I often worried about her. There was a few times she had come to school with bruises on her wrists that revealed themselves when she reached for something in the book corner, when I confronted her about them she claimed she had gotten them from a fight she had with her sister, it didn't sit well with me but I took her word for it, the next day she was more cautious with her sleeves. This day was different though, she bounded into class with a spring in her step offering me a smile as she passed, it was the first time I had seen her where she wasn't falling asleep at her desk.

"Good morning Wynter!"
"Morning Miss Larkin!"

Wynter had been referred to the school psychologist a few times, but her parents had never responded to any letters so nothing further could be done but perhaps things were finally looking up for her.

"Alright class, get your English notebooks out, we are going to do some creative writing today…"

The class groaned, most of them hated creative writing but I liked reading what they'd write.

"Think of something in your life right now that makes you happy, write about that, you have one hour, any questions, hands up…" The class fell silent as every single child got their head down and began to write. This was my favourite grade to teach, they wanted to be older than they were yet they still had their child like innocence, they were inquisitive and were just finding their opinions. It was a fun age to teach.

When break time rolled around, the class rushed out to the yard for recess and I gathered up their creative writing pieces.

"Knock knock!"

I turned around to find Lara at the door, she entered and sat herself down in my desk chair and spun it around.

"hey!"

"I just wanted to pick your brain about something..."

"ooooh, I'm intrigued..."

"So I was speaking to Wynter Jones during art class, were you aware her mother had passed away?"

"I wasn't aware, do you know if there's a dad in the picture?"

"Unsure... She's a strange one..."

"she sure is" I placed the creative writing pieces on my desk and turned to face Lara "I honestly don't know too much about her, she's always very well behaved, I have never had to contact her guardians for anything, well, I know she has been referred to the school psychologist but no one has ever responded to the referral permitting it..."

"just keep an eye on it... I had to send her to keep her back after class for kicking one of the easels"

"Really? That's not like Wynter at all..."

"That's when she told me about her mother."

Lara had been super vigilant since the death of a student that she knew due to abuse, she noticed things that perhaps I wouldn't even think to notice.

"Do you think I should contact her parents to arrange a meeting?"

"Do you have a reason to?"

"I'm not sure..." I thought "I guess not..."

"Just take extra care with her...."

I nodded, thinking about Lara's concerns, wondering if there was anything to them.

I spent that night after putting my daughter to bed reading through Wynter's creative writing piece to see if it raised any alarm bells. She wrote about how she had made a new friend, how she was strange but nice, how she never really had that many friends so it was nice to have one. The girl's name was Violet and she was home-schooled, her father was strict but only because he cared about her. I could feel myself smiling because I could sense her happiness through the page, I rarely saw Wynter smile, but perhaps this new friend was all she needed, perhaps she was lonely. I rested my head down on my pillow, turned the bedside light off and drifted off to sleep.

WYNTER

I wasn't scared of many things, I wasn't scared of the dark, of spiders of snakes, I wasn't scared of the bogey man or heights, I wasn't even scared of the dentist but there was one thing that gave me cold sweats, made me tremble and caused my heart to beat like a drum through my chest whenever I even thought of it and that was being left on my own. When I was four years old my mother would leave me for days in the tiny box apartment that we used to live in before my mother inherited our house from her mother. I'd sit for hours by the door waiting for her to come home, that's why I was so relieved when Alma was born, I had someone to keep me company on those long testing nights, even if that person couldn't speak to me, I could speak to her, and I did, I told her of my fears, goals, wants, how one day I'd get a really good job and enough money that she'd never want for anything, I wanted to provide her with a different childhood experience than I had.

"Wynter, Wynter, wake up!"
I was awakened to the sound of my sisters voice and the feeling of her pinching my arm.

"What is it Alma"

"My daddy's here"

My worst fear was about to come true; I was about to be alone. You see, Alma, Cleo and I had different fathers, Alma's father, Mark, was an engineer, he was happily married and had two other kids, a boy and a girl, Emma and Jack, Cleo's father Samuel owned a bar on the main strip in Charlotte, he had an older daughter, Carley. who had left to go to university in California and he had all the time in the world for Cleo, if he didn't live on the other side of North Carolina I knew he'd see her every day, and every time he came to see Cleo he brought her something. My father was non-existent, according to my mother, he was either her ex who is now in jail or the one who overdosed, either way it was a lose lose situation. Once a month, Almas' father and Cleos' father would take them for the weekend and I'd be left either alone or with my mother, but with the latter I might as well have just been by myself.

"Morning Wynter, have you gotten taller?"
Mark had perched himself down on the couch at the very edge as if he was too afraid to sit fully on it.

"You ought to get your eyes checked Marky Mark, haven't grown since I was like eight"
Alma sat down on her father's lap and wrapped herself in his arms, he kissed her head, I was so happy that my sister had some sort of temporary escape, I just wished I did too. Outside the sound of a car engine drew to a halt, it was Samuel, he let himself in, the first thing he did on entry was scoop Cleo who was sitting by the door like she always did when she knew he was coming up into a big bear hug. Right on queue, my mother appeared from her bedroom, still dressed from the night before, hair shoved carelessly into a messy bun and mascara trailing down her cheeks.

"Mark, Sam…" She announced, going into the kitchen she grabbed a glass from the cupboard and filled it with water before gulping it down. Every time my mother knew that her ex's were coming she made sure to hide the beer bottles and any evidence that proved her to be an unfit mother, though it would have taken a lot more than that, I was sure Mark and Samuel could see through her façade.

"Good to see you again Lyric." Mark lied, according to him, when he broke it off with my mother, she threw a

hair dryer at his head and gave him a concussion.
"Daddy, daddy, can we go?"
"Sure thing Ali"
Mark lifted Alma high up onto his shoulders, he was tall, like a giant, everything was big, his head, his hands, his feet, he was like a real life "big friendly giant" from a book I had read once.
"Yeah, we better get going too" Samuel announced.
"I'll have Alma back first thing Sunday morning"
"Same here"
I watched them leave, closing the door behind them, through the window I watched them drive away, it wasn't until I saw them disappear into the distance that I truly felt alone.

"Hey, squirt, why don't we watch a movie tonight?" I hadn't left the window since my sisters had left me that morning and my mother had been watching me, I could feel her eyes burning into me as she lit up her first cigarette then her second and then her third, I turned my gaze from the window to her, she was sitting on the couch, she had wiped the makeup off from under her eyes, she seemed almost normal. I climbed down from the windowsill and sheepishly made my way to the couch; she reached out her arms to me. "C'mon Wynie, it'll be just like old times, we can watch the nutcracker, like we did when you were little"
I actually hated the nutcracker, I found it dull and boring, but it was my mothers favourite film and she hadn't been this involved in my life since I came out of the womb so I nodded. Our television was tiny and was like something from the 80's, with the VCR and the pixelated screen, but non the less, my mother popped the video in and we snuggled up on the couch, it had been a long time since my mother showed me any type of affection, she had never been that type of mother, the type to wrap you up

in her arms when you got hurt, or tell you it was okay whenever it felt like the world was ending, she was more of a, let you do your own thing type of mother, a don't get in the way and we'll get along just fine type of mother but I knew she cared about me, in her own, unique way.

"Mama..." I pulled myself from her arms and turned fully to face her. "Why doesn't my dad come and visit me?"
She spent way too long thinking, so I knew that she was conjuring up a lie in her head.

"He's a busy guy, your dad..."
When my mother lied, her nose twitched, that was the first clue, the second clue was that her mouth was open and words were coming out. I sank into the couch longing for the thick black leather to swallow me up and take me to another dimension, a dimension where darkness didn't exist, it was sunny all the time, and people were happy, there was no reason not to be, I knew it was just a pipe dream, but that didn't stop me from hoping.

That night I laid alone on the mattress that was only big enough for one but somehow we always managed to squeeze on three, even with all the space it just didn't feel right without Cleo stirring and Alma talking in her sleep, for the first time ever, I felt truly afraid in my own home. I heard the sound of the front door clicking closed, and then the hushed voices of my mother and whatever male companion she had brought home this time, I heard them tiptoe through the living room though it wasn't so quiet as they seemed to bump into every single thing they passed, I heard the creak of them opening and closing the door to my mother's bedroom that was right next to mine and the walls were thin and then I heard the rhythm of the bedsprings. I grabbed my dusty old pillow and wrapped it around my head to cover my ears and I began to count, something I did every time I was trying to distract myself, 1… 2… 3… I pictured myself in a field, running through the wheat… 4… 5… 6… Flowers surrounded me as the fresh breeze blew through my hair… 7… 8… 9… I was running towards an aqua coloured ocean, the waves crashing up onto the rocks, the sound like music to my ears… 10… 11… 12… It wasn't working, I opened my eyes and I was still in my cramped little bedroom, alone.

Dawn broke through the sky like my mother's heart when boyfriend number 4 cheated on her, I hadn't slept a wink, outside my window a thick mist was stuck in the atmosphere, if I hadn't known any better, I'd have thought it was smoke. For a moment I just sat motionless, gazing out the window, nothing breathed, everything was silent, the only thing moving was the light as it travelled to become fully illuminate. I crawled off of the mattress, my bones heavy, before heaving them to the upright position, and made my way to the kitchen to relieve my rumbling stomach.

"Morning." I was met with the sight of a grown man wearing only a vest and his boxershorts. "You must be Wynter"
The man was a clear head taller than people that I would have considered tall, he was bulky, with muscular arms and I was sure he had a six pack beneath that vest, his face was clean shaven, and it was obvious that he took pride in his looks. My mother breezed joyfully out of her room and to the kitchen by his side, I was still glued to the spot, my feet not allowing me to move, I wasn't sure if it was because I was so beyond exhausted or that I had seen this scene before, my mother would bring a man home and he'd be the only man in the world for her, she'd talk of marriage, maybe a few more kids (Like she didn't already have enough) and then he'd leave her without a word and she'd revert to her original form, a

broken shell of a woman, it was a vicious cycle, one that I had become accustomed to.

"Wynter, this is Dominic..." It made me sick the way she danced her fingers up and down his arm and nibbled on his ear, the way he grabbed her by the hips and pulled her into him, I had lost track of what boyfriend number this one was.

"Nice to meet you Wynter" He crouched down to my height in a way that can only be described as condescending. "What a pretty little girl you are"
All of a sudden, I had lost my appetite, I nodded my head and began to make for the door.

"Hey Wynter, where you going?"

"Out..."

"No you aren't" Great, she chose a wonderful time to start acting like a parent. "I thought we could spend the morning together, just the three of us before Alma and Cleo come home." She didn't see me roll my eyes because I had my back to her but I rolled them so far back I was sure they'd disappear into my sockets. I plastered a smile on my face and pivoted round to where my mother and her new man candy still stood. "Good girl." She praised me, like a dog.

"Why don't we make breakfast together, Wynter, I heard you like to cook..." Nodding gently, my teeth gritted so hard my gums were beginning to hurt, I moved towards Dominic, who was already rummaging in the cupboards to see what we had, he was going to get the shock of his life when he realised that we had very little that was edible. "I know, why don't we go out for breakfast." This was new, I didn't remember a time where my mother's bit on the side invited me to go out with them, most of them just pretended I didn't exist or didn't even know about me, I smiled, but this time it was real.

Dominic took us to a cute little café that sat near the pier overlooking the fishermen and their boats, though it was winter so there wasn't many out. We were greeted at the door by a waitress who was wearing an old-fashioned black dress and white apron and had her hair styled like one of the women from the old movies I used to watch with my Granma, she sat us in a booth by the window. I had never been somewhere quite like this before, it was an old quaint 50's diner style with black and white checkers flooring and wooden counters that looked like they were going to fall apart, but still I found it beautiful, almost charming.

"You can order anything you want off the menu Wynter…" Dominic announced as the waitress placed the menus in front of us, the options were endless, pancakes topped with maple syrup, waffles smothered in whipped cream and sprinkles, bacon and eggs, big plates of them, in the end I went with the pancakes, my mother and Dominic both ordered chocolate covered croissants. "So Wynter, your mama tells me you love to dance?"

"I haven't danced since I was 5 years old and she pulled me out because we couldn't afford lessons." I felt the thud of a boot against my ankle under the table and read my mother's reaction, maybe I wasn't supposed to say that. "But still, I love it… Mama and I love to watch the nutcracker together"

"It's Wynters' favourite movie"
It really wasn't but my mother didn't know me at all evidently so often I just went along with her narrative just to keep the peace.

"Hey Wynter, why don't we go over there and spend some of my money in that games machine." Dominic nodded towards the old style illuminous orange machine that stood by the door, I looked to my mother pleadingly and when she nodded I jumped up out of my seat and we made our way over to the machine, I hated to admit it but I liked Dominic, he was kind, seemed to care about me and my mother and appeared to have his head screwed on, I was starting to wonder what the catch was. Dominic inserted a coin into the slot and we began to play, I wasn't very good but he always encouraged me to try again. In talking to him I found out he was a heart doctor, that he also volunteered with sick children and that he had two dogs called Buzz and Woody, in other words, he was way too good for my mother...

After demolishing my mountain of pancakes, Dominic took us to the frozen lake about a 20-minute drive outside of Sherwood. It's where most people flocked to during the Winter months since there wasn't a real ice rink for miles. It was packed and I couldn't help wondering how such thin ice could hold so many bodies without giving in, just another way in which the world worked in mysterious ways. I had never ice skated before so I couldn't control my legs and I spent more time on my butt than on my feet but I had fun, eventually, Dominic gave in and decided to lift me as he glided along the surface so effortlessly all the while my mother was clinging on to him trying to keep herself upright. This was the first time I had ever felt like a normal family, the first time I saw my mother really laugh, the first time I didn't feel like I was being crushed by the weight of the world, I felt free.

Alma and Cleo arrived home at the exact same time, 3PM on the dot on Sunday ambushing me on arrival with hugs until we all fell back onto the concrete before bounding inside hand in hand.

"Wynter I missed you!" Alma yelled smothering me as she wrapped her arms tight around my neck.

"I missed you too Al... And You Cleo..." I

scooped an unsuspecting Cleo into my arms as she squealed and giggled, there was something so beautiful about their innocence, an innocence that I had never had and sometimes wished that I did, they were so unaware that the world wasn't all sunshine and roses, sometimes I used my sisters as my escape as a way to hold onto the tiny spec of childhood that I had left. "Did you have fun at your dads?"

"So much fun, he took me to the fayre and I won a goldfish, it's living at his house though, it's called Bob, I wish you could have come Wynie…"

"I wished I could have too, but I did have fun here, mama has a new boyfriend"

"Great…" Alma said sarcastically, a tone she had learned from me, regrettably,

"No, no, this one's different, he's, nice, kind"
Alma raised her eyebrows in surprise, at 5 years old she had learned that our mother didn't have the best taste in men, a lesson that came to all who lived in the Jones house at one point or another.

"can we do something fun Wynter?"

"Sure, what do you want to do?"

"Park?"

"Okay but only for a little while, you need to get dinner and an early night for school tomorrow"

"I don't want to go to school."

"Alma, you have to, plus, you love school!"

"Not anymore…"

"what's going on?" Alma's smile quickly faded and she turned her head away from me, scooting out of my reach. "Alma is someone bothering you?"

"I don't want to talk about it, okay?"

"Alma, it might help…"
She sighed, turning back towards me.

"It's just some girls, they say I smell and my clothes

are ugly, do I smell Wynter?"
I grabbed her and pulled her into me, I remembered experiencing the exact same thing at her age, being sent to school with dirty clothes, unbathed, and I had tried my best to stop in from happening to Alma, but it seemed that I had failed.

"No, you don't smell Al..." I rested my chin on her head.

"Then why do they say it?" She looked up to me for reassurance, I flattened the baby hairs sticking out of her loose ponytail.

"Because kids can be mean" I told her "just ignore them, you have more personality in your little finger than all those girls put together."

"Really?"

"of course, but you do need to go to school, because if you let a bunch of mean girls wreck your future, then they've won and my little Ali cat is smarter than that, besides, you're my sister, you must have some toughness in ya..."

Alma buried her head into me and I cradled her in my arms, Cleo mimicked the motion, wrapping her chubby arms around Alma, I always found it funny how infants just knew when you were feeling down and they knew to try and help make you feel better, though it was the first time I had ever seen Cleo with any clear understanding of what was going on. Alma fell asleep with her head on my chest that night whilst I sat gazing out the window pondering my thoughts. I thought about my mother and her new relationship with Dominic, how he was too good for her and my fear that he'd break her heart and we'd be right back where we started, I thought about Violet, how wonderfully strange she was, yet she seemed so vulnerable and breakable, like she'd snap in half if you pushed her over and how she held her cards so close to her chest that you never fully knew her, what she'd experienced, what her life was like and I thought about how I'd told my teacher that my mother had died and how unbelievably guilty I felt that the thought had even crossed my mind.

VIOLET

Every single day I watched Wynter and her sister walking home from school, I'd wave to her and she'd wave back and keep on walking, I wondered where she'd go, where she lived, what it was like. So, one day, after she had passed and we had exchanged our waves, I snuck out through the fence and followed her. I followed her down the street and around the corner to a street full of one-story houses, half the size of my own, with white picket fences, she entered a house on the end, I moved closer to get a better look and went around to the back of the house where I saw Wynter preparing dinner for her siblings, feeding her baby sister and rocking her to sleep, as if she was her mother. The house was messy and undecorated. I watched for several minutes before heading back home. I often wondered what my life would be like if my real parents had kept me, would I go to school? Would I have siblings to fight with and play with? Would we go on family days out? These were the things I dreamt about.

My father arrived home in the dead of night, I heard him sneak into my room, he stroked my face with the back of my hand and sat on the floor and watched me sleep, or at least, pretend to sleep. It was only when I heard him rise to his feet, walk up the stairs and creak the door closed, that I could finally drift off into my slumber, I could never really fully drift off though, I was always on edge, always prepared, always half awake. When I woke up the next morning he was working out in his office, doing pull ups on his pull up bar, I entered the room and he stopped to take a swig of his water.
"morning father."
He nodded his head to me then continued his pull ups.

My father was built like a brick house with arms the size of tree trunks.
"Can I ask a question?"
"Can it wait?" He scoffed abruptly.
I shuffled on the spot; he rolled his eyes and turned his full attention to me.
"What were my parents like?"
"Useless, couldn't take care of a kid even if they wanted to…"
"what did they do for jobs?"
"How should I know?"
"Do you think they wonder how I am?"
"What's with the third-degree Violet? You should really be grateful for what you have…"
"Yes, sir."
I retreated from the room feeling defeated and began my daily jobs, first scrubbing the floors, starting with the kitchen, then the lounge, next the bathroom and lastly my father's room, I used the same old rag and a pale of soapy water that I used most days, I often wondered what the point was, then I remembered, my father didn't need a reason to punish me, simply breathing was enough some days, next was to clean the toilet, that was my least favourite job as sometimes my father forgot to flush, my father said chores helped to keep my mind active and kept me out of trouble, it seemed like most days I was in trouble though.

After I was sure my father was asleep that night, I snuck out again, like I did most nights now to watch Wynter and her sisters through the window. I wasn't exactly sure what I would do if I got caught but I felt so hopeful watching them, they had virtually nothing and seemed happy, maybe I could be happy too. I felt a single tear fall down my cheek, I was shivering in the cold but so fixated I couldn't bring myself to leave so I stayed for a while, until I knew they were asleep and I walked home. I crept past my father's room, the floorboards shrieking, I heard him stir, I closed my eyes tightly, maybe he didn't hear me, maybe, just maybe, but I was wrong, I felt the breeze of this door swinging open and, dressed in nothing but his boxer shorts he appeared in the doorway, he grabbed me by the wrist so tightly my hand had begun to turn purple and was throbbing and that's when I felt it, the blow to my stomach and then another to my nose causing my head to fall back so hard, I thought it may fall right off. My vision blurred and my head felt fuzzy, like I was in a dream and I felt him drag me down the stairs to be basement, not letting go of my wrist that now felt so fragile it appeared to be on the verge of breaking, I knew then what was going to happen, confinement. Normally I would have kicked and screamed and made a fuss but I didn't have the energy, I was like a dead weight the only thing holding me up was my father, he removed the rug and opened the door and dropped me in like a piece of rubbish, the cold clinging to my skin like a leaf to a tree.

"You never learn, I ought to get rid of you, you little brat!"

He slammed the door shut and locked it. I sat down on the ground that was so cold that it felt wet, pulled my knees into my chest and rested my chin on them, sometimes, I wished that things were different, I knew I deserved it, I had broken the rules but I just wished I was born into a different life.

I didn't sleep a wink that night and the next day my father didn't bring me food, my stomach was in agony and I wasn't sure if it was due to the punch or the hunger, either way it wasn't very pleasant. A is for apple, B is for book, C is for cake, D is for dog, E is for elephant… A is for apple, B is for book, C is for cake, D is for dog, E is for elephant… There were 12 cracks in the walls in total, I dreamed about shrinking really small, so small that I could fit right through one of the cracks. A is for apple, B is for book, C is for cake, D is for dog, E is for elephant... I picked up a pebble from the side and began etching my writing into the wall, my father had torn up my book so I didn't know what came next but I was holding out hope for Wynter to teach me. Day 2 of confinement, I still hadn't eaten and I was starting to feel slightly weak, all I did that day was lie on the ground and count the bricks on the walls but Wynter had only taught me to count to 20 so I just counted to 20 over and over again.

"You are my sunshine, my only sunshine." I sang softly, my voice echoing off of the walls. "You make me happy when skies are grey" I could hear the birds outside chirping cheerfully, if I could be any animal I'd be a bird, free to fly anywhere I wanted anytime I wanted. "You'll never know dear, how much I love you..." I wondered if Wynter would come looking for me like she did before, if she even knew I was missing. "Please don't take my sunshine away. Day 3 of confinement, my father brought me a small glass of water and two slices of white bread before leaving and locking the door again, I demolished it in seconds, I slept most of that day, and then day 4 came, I could barely get myself off of the ground when I heard the sound of the dead bolt unlocking and my father appeared at the top of the ladder, he climbed down, lifted me over his shoulder and placed me on the camp bed in the basement, he forced a straw into my mouth that was inside a glass of water and told me to drink, I did as I was told. My body was aching but I managed to sit up.

"That's my girl..." My father ran his hands softly through my hair in a way that made me feel uncomfortable. "Why don't you get some rest, I brought you some soup, to get your strength up." He handed me a bowl filled with rich tomato soup, the heat from the bowl warming my hands and thawing them, he kissed my forehead before retreating upstairs as I scooped each delightful spoonful of soup into my mouth. I heard my father leave for work.

    Although I was still weak, I wanted to see Wynter, I wanted her to know I was okay. My father would be gone for a while and I would be back before he even knew I was gone. I heaved my heavy bones out of bed and limped up the stairs and stepped out into the cold. I hobbled my weak body down the street to Wynter's house, I just needed to see her.

WYNTER

The next time that I saw Violet was in the most unexpected of ways, I had tucked my sisters into bed, kissed them good night and retreated to my nightly routine of gazing out the window counting the stars and taking the time to be by myself, something that very rarely happened, when I saw the silhouette of a young girl, sitting across the road from my house, staring up at me, I wasn't sure if she could see me since it was pitch black but I watched her for several moments before deciding to head out to see her, I clambered over Cleo and Alma who were sleeping like logs, crept through the living room and out the door, hugged onto the house as I made my way to the back and there she was, I could see her clearer now, partially illuminated by the silver moonlight. She was shaking like a leaf, her hands gripping the opposing forearms, barefoot as always.

"Violet?" She jumped at the sound of her name, maybe she hadn't seen me, I grew closer. "What are you doing here?"
She looked up at me, the sight almost knocked me over like a gust of wind, half of her face seemed normal, beautiful, like a porcelain doll, the other half was black and blue starting from her eyebrow right down to her chin no space was unharmed, she also had slight bruising on her wrists, she was in bad shape.

"Violet, what happened?" I knelt down beside her and placed a hand on her shoulder, she shook me off abruptly and turned her face away, but it was too late, I had already seen.

"A few days ago, I followed you home, I wanted to see where you lived, see if it was as bad as you said it was" She chuckled to herself "it is, but I've been coming here every night since, you take such good care of your sisters, like you take care of me"

"But your face?"

"you're such a good friend Wynter, I never had a friend before you.. Promise you won't ever leave me, that we will be best friends forever." Violet began to well up, the tears waterfalling from her eyes and down her cheeks.

"Violet!" I grabbed her by both shoulders and shook her towards me. "Snap out of it, what happened to you, you face…?"

"Confinement."

"What's confinement?"

Without saying another word, Violet collapsed in my arms like she couldn't bear her own weight anymore, I rested my chin on her head and rocked her back and forth and back and forth all the while racking my brains for an explanation, but Violet rarely did explain herself, in the grand scheme of things, I didn't really know this girl at all, she was like a stranger to me, yet I felt like I had known her my whole life. I walked her home in silence that night where she slipped through the gap in the fence and began on her way but before she disappeared around the corner, she turned around to face me.

"I meant what I said Wynter"

"What?"

"you're a great friend"

She offered me a meek smile before fading into the darkness, I waited for a moment, not sure what I was waiting for but for some odd reason my feet couldn't move, I saw the porch light turn on and she disappeared inside.

The walk home seemed much longer than usual and my thoughts were plaguing my brain like a dark cloud encroaching in on blue skies.

"Wynter Olivia Jones, where the hell have you been?" A voice immediately cleared my head, that voice was my mothers, and she was standing in the middle of the living room with her hands on her hips when I entered the house, busted, she picked a strange time to start mothering me. "I've been worried sick, do you know how late it is"

"I'm aware…"

I could smell the strong scent of alcohol coming from her from where I was standing, it was attacking my nostrils, I walked past her not expecting her reflexes to be as quick as they were and she swivelled around, not lifting her feet off the ground and grabbed me by the wrist.

"Don't walk away from me when I'm talking to you!"

"Sh! You'll wake the kids…"

"I'm the mother here"

She was slurring her words and trying really hard to stay upright and I, quite frankly, was not in the mood to deal with her, I was getting used to her being sober but I knew sooner or later she'd find her way back to the bottle, my mother never stayed clean for long, the longest she had ever gone without alcohol in my existence was one month and that was when she dated Cleos' dad, he didn't drink, couldn't stand the stuff, she couldn't even stop when she was pregnant with Cleo and Alma.

"Mama, why don't we put you to bed?"

My mother nodded her head, draping herself around my neck, her whole weight pressing down on top of me as I stumbled into her bedroom, desperately trying to keep my balance before dumping her in a heap on her bed.

"you take care of me Wynter…"

"Yeah, I know, now let's get you tucked in"

I forced her limp legs beneath the duvet and tucked it right up under her chin, I sat down on the edge of her bed and began to stroke her hair, it's how I used to get her to sleep when she'd have her off days.

"Wynter... Men suck... You're better off just staying away from them."

"Well, at least Dominic isn't like other guys, he's nice, he treats you right, he really does love you, I can tell."

"that's over Wynter."

The words stabbed through me like a knife, painful, then came the anger, bubbling up from my toes all the way through my body ready to erupt like a volcano.

"What did you do?!"

"Wynter..."

"He was perfect and you went and ruined it, like you ruin everything else!"

It was like a demon had possessed me; I had never spoken to my mother like this before but I couldn't control it.

"You don't know what you're talking about"

"you just can't keep your legs closed can you?"

"Wynter I'm pregnant"

I felt my jaw drop to the floor and the weight of the world was suddenly crushing my bones, the room began to spin, I was floating on a cloud, up in the sky, surrounded by rainbows and green fields filled with daisies, Violet was there and Alma and Cleo and Dominic and Miss Giles and Miss Larkin but as the world began to spin faster and faster they faded and everything went black.

I woke up on the freezing cold wooden floor of the living room, it was lighter than I had last remembered, I blinked hard trying to make the world fade into focus before sitting up, it was eerily quiet, like someone had died. Maybe I had died? On the windowsill sat my mother, her arms wrapped around her knees on which she rested her chin. Slowly, I rose to my feet, still dizzy, she didn't even flinch, I began to move my feet, they were stiff as wood, still, nothing.

"Mama?" I managed, my throat was dry so it came

out croaky, I knew she heard me because her eyes widened, but she didn't respond. "Mama..."
"You've been out for 5 hours"
"Did I faint?"
My mother nodded, swivelling her body towards me so that she now had her back to the window, she seemed to have sobered up.
"I told you I was pregnant and then you were out like a light."
I had hoped it was a dream, I had hoped she wasn't procreating when she couldn't even take care of the kids that she already had, I had hoped that the whole conversation had never happened.
"Is Dominic the dad?" She shrugged, unbothered, like she hadn't just turned all of our lives upside down, I could feel the rage coming back but I breathed deeply to diffuse it, my ears were ringing and my head was pounding. I sat myself down on the couch. "How can you not know? Are you seriously that much of a slut?"
"Where did you learn that word?"
"When you raise yourself you pick up on a few things..."
"Wynter, I'm really not in the mood, so can you save the lecture?"
"No, we're doing this now." I took a deep breath "Are you going to have it?"
"the baby?" she nodded, much to my dismay, "Yeah..."
A crushing feeling inside my chest weighed down on my heart like a thousand rocks were being piled on top of me.
"You can't keep it, where will it sleep? There's barely even enough room for the four of us... I can't take care of another baby I just can't!!!"
Before I knew it, my fury had sprung to life and I was standing right in front of her, trembling, the sweat pouring

from my brow, rage flowing through my bones like lava and without another word I took myself to the bedroom barely noticing Cleo and Alma who were holding one another in the corner and I broke down, falling to my knees, layers of sadness and anger and confusion piled deep into my soul, my eyes rimmed with tears but I couldn't fight them anymore, they fell from my eyes like crystals and then I felt it, the impact of Alma's arms wrapping me up like a warm safe blanket, for the first time in her life, I was unable to tell her that everything was going to be okay, because I simply didn't know.

When I was three years old my Granma took me to the fayre, I remembered the colours so vividly, the bright lights, the stalls, the loud music, the people. My Grandmother lifted me onto her shoulders to see everything more clearly, the fayre went on for miles, I couldn't even see its end.

"How about we try to win you something?" My Granma whispered as she placed me onto the ground and we approached a games stall, the aim was to knock over the milk bottles, my Granma tried first, only managing 2 bottles, then I tried, missing completely.

"Alright, Wynter, last go, blow on the ball, for luck"

I rubbed the plastic ball on my pink cardigan and gave it a blow before launching it with all my might, smack, all the bottles came tumbling down and my Granma cheered swinging me around, I picked the gigantic monkey, my mother pawned it 3 weeks later to buy cigarettes. This memory with my Granma often popped into my head in times of distress, up until her death when I was 6 years old, she was my one and only ally. Alma emerged from the bedroom, she had fixed her own hair and picked her own outfit, Alma was very emotionally intelligent, she knew exactly when I needed time to breathe, when I didn't have the energy, this was one of those days.

"Wynter, can I share the last banana with Cleo?"

"Yeah, but hurry up, we've got to get going to school" Alma unpeeled the banana, halved it and gave the other half to Cleo and began eating her own half. "Alright, let's go"

I lifted Cleo onto my hip, we dropped her off with Caroline and proceeded to Alma's school.

"Keep your head up today, okay? Don't let anyone push you around." I pulled Alma into a big bear hug, kissing her head and watched her skip onto the playground before I headed to my own school. I met Genevieve by the school gate, she pursed her lips before approaching me.

"Hey, I'm sorry about what I said about your mama…"

"it's okay…"

"Hey, are you alright, you seem, down."

"I'm fine." I lied "Same old same old…"

"Hey, I was wondering if you'd want to come over to mine this weekend, I'm having a little get together with some girls."

It wasn't really my thing but Genevieve was extending an Olive branch so I had to take it, I nodded.

"Sure, can I bring a friend?"

"Yeah, the more the merrier."

VIOLET

"What's a party?"

"Well, it's not really a party more of a small get together..." she paused, catching my eye, "You've never been to a party?"

I shook my head. Wynter split her ham sandwich and passed me half through the bars in the fence along with a new spelling book, gleefully I began flicking through the book before turning my attention back to Wynter.

"I'm not sure Wynter, what if I get caught" I broke a piece of the sandwich and shovelled it into my mouth.

"It'll just be a couple of hours... Won't your dad want you to have fun?"

"He's not really the fun type, more the one who disciplines when I break the rules"

"Please Violet, don't make me beg, it'll be fun, and we'll have you back before your dad even notices you're gone." She didn't know the half of it, my father would know, he always knew. "You can come to mines before and get something to wear, I reckon we're about the same size..." She looked from my eyes down to my feet "And some shoes..."

I had never had shoes and my father only bought me a new dress when the one I had got so skin tight that I couldn't physically breathe. I wanted so badly to be like Wynter, free to roam wherever she wanted, sometimes it felt like I was in a prison.

"Alright..." I sighed

"Alright?" A thin smile crept onto Wynter's face, "You're coming?"

I nodded and Wynter began to jump up and down with delight and I was left wondering if I has made the correct decision.

When Saturday came, I had my biggest challenge ever, getting out of the house without getting caught. My father lay sprawled across the couch, a bowl of cheese puffs in hand, eyes glued to the television. I peered at him from the top of the basement stairs as he shovelled each mouthful in, leaving remnants of orange dust on his fingertips. I slipped into the hallway, still fixated on my father and what his next move may be, thinking about what would happen if I got caught, a week in confinement? Maybe a month? Or maybe worse. Maybe he'd bury me in the garden like he had threatened to do before, or cut off my hands like he warned me he'd do one time for sneaking food. I took a deep breath and wandered into the living room, where he was, cleared my throat and quietly spoke.

"Is there anything you need done today?"

My father raised one of his eyebrows in surprise and sat up.

"You're asking for work?"

"Well, I noticed the leaves at the back of the house could do with being raked…"

"How did you notice that?"

Shoot, I gulped, attempting to keep my cool.

"Well…" I paused "When I was, um, bad the other day and you put me in confinement, I could kind of see out the little window in there…"

"I see…" He seemed sceptical "are you lying to me Violet?"

My father rose to his feet, placing his bowl down onto the couch, now towering over me, he grabbed my ear with his massive hands and began to pull slightly, the pain immense.

"No, I promise!"

"Because if you are, there's a perfectly good hole at the back of this house, you might just find

yourself there." He let go of my ear, leaving a sharp throbbing sensation. He sighed and turned his back. "Fine, I'm heading out for a few hours for work, when I come back, that garden better be the best it's ever looked" I nodded, paralysed with fear, unable to speak. "Go".
I ran to the door, opened it and sped out, I signalled to Wynter who was standing on the other side of the fence, she squeezed through the gap in the fence, and darted towards me, following me around to the back of the house.
"Did he buy it?"
"I'm not sure." I told her honestly.
"Let's get this done then…"
I handed Wynter a rake that I had gotten from the shed and we both began the task that I had promised my father.

    Wynter and I stepped back to admire our work, I noticed her smile, it was pretty, like flowers, she didn't do it too often but when she did it made me smile also. Before I could say anything she has taken my hand and we both squeezed back through the fence and ran down the street to her house. She put her finger to her lip and shushed me before peering into the house, her mother was lying on the couch, snoring like a warthog, worse than fathers snoring. I followed Wynter through to her room, it was small but it wasn't a basement. On the bed asleep was Wynters younger sister, she was thin and looked like she'd break if you hugged her too hard, she was sleeping soundly, peacefully. Wynter picked up a blanket and draped it over her tentatively.

    "She's been unwell these past few days,,," Wynter told me "Been sleeping a lot, when she's not crying… But I can't get her medicine because we can't afford it…"
Wynter picked up a pile of clothes from the corner of the room and began lying them out on the floor in front of me.

"Anything take your fancy Violet?" I thought for a moment, scanning my options before pointing to a pink frilly dress with polka dots that she had paired with a purple headband and beaded bracelet, Wynter smiled as she picked up the clothes and handed them to me. "Go try them on…"

I took the clothes and began to remove my clothing to replace my own, that's when Wynter took hold of my arm.

"What are those bruises from?" She took a step back, examining me, it made me uncomfortable to I hurriedly pulled the dress she had given me over my head, It was slightly loose but was as good a fit as it was going to be.

"I'm just clumsy…"

"Violet…"

"Seriously, I bump into everything, trip over all the time, it's no biggie" I put on all my accessories. "What do you think?" I posed like one of the cat walk models I had seen pictured in one of my father's magazines. Wynter laughed.

"You look beautiful…"

"Really?"

"Yes, you can keep the dress…"

"I can?" I could feel my face lighting up.

"Yeah, it looks better on you than it ever did on me…"

I threw my arms around Wynter and pulled her into a hug, she was like a sister to me, no one had ever treated me the way Wynter Jones did.

"We need shoes!" Wynter ran out of the room and came back in with sparkly purple pumps. "These are perfect, they're my little sister Alma's, they should fit, I think your feet are quite a bit smaller than mines…"

I took the shoes in my hands, they were the most beautiful

things I had ever seen. I put them down and slid my feet into them, they were the perfect fit, I felt like a princess for the first time ever, I felt pretty for the first time ever.

    Wynter and I spent the rest of the morning getting ready, she brushed my hair out and curled in with her mother's magic curling thingy, she even borrowed her mother's lipstick and put that on me too, when I looked in the mirror, I didn't even recognise myself and oddly, I liked that, I got to feel like someone else for the day, I got to feel normal.

    "Wynnie, can I come with you today?" Alma, who had come back from her friend's house asked as Wynter tried to make her feel included by curling her hair like she had mine.

    "No Alma, it's a big girl party" Wynter paused "But if you want, when I get back, we can get cuddled up and I'll make up a story for you..."
Alma beamed, I really looked up to Wynter and admired her, she was truly amazing, I so wished that I was born into her family, was one of her sisters, they seemed happy, it wasn't easy for them but they had each other, I didn't have anyone but my father, is it wrong to want more?

    Wynter walked slightly ahead of me as we made our way to her friend's house. It seemed like Wynter's friend was quite well off, her house was large and painted yellow and the lawn had a multitude of stone sculptures and a bird bath. Wynter knocked on the door, she seemed to be nervous, she kept on tugging at her ears and rocking on her feet from side to side. All of a sudden the door opened and a woman answered, I assumed the girl's mother, she had a kind face with dimples of her cheeks and large inviting eyes with dark hair that was shoved into a tight ponytail, I had never had a mother but if I could choose one, I'd have picked her.

"Oh hello Wynter, who's your friend?" The woman asked.

"This is Violet..."

"Nice to meet you Violet, well the girls are out back, why don't you girls go out and join them?" The woman moved to one side, allowing us to walk past, the inside of the house was just as grand as the outside, the pictures on the wall told the story of a happy family, a mother a father two girls and a boy, the mother and father seemed very much in love as they smiled in their wedding pictures then again at the birth of each of their children, I wondered what it was like, to have a normal life, a normal family, uncomplicated.

"Wynter!" Called a girl from the back of the gigantic garden, I guessed it was her party. We made our way over to the girls who were all sitting on a pink checkered blanket, drinks in hand and an abundance of snacks in bowls, mostly foods I had never even seen before. The whole prospect was foreign to me, I had never even had one friend, let alone socialised with a bunch of girls like this.

"Hey G, this is my friend Violet... Violet this is Genevieve, Riley, Orla and G's cousins Brenna and Rose..."

"Hi Violet, I love your dress" The girl they called Genevieve commented, I could feel my face burning red.

"Thank you, Wynter let me borrow it, I only have one dress and it's kind of old now..." I could see the girls puzzled looks but I couldn't understand why. Genevieve handed me a pink cup filled with pink liquid, I lifted it to my nose to smell, it smelled sweet.

"It's fruit punch, haven't you ever had fruit punch before?" I shook my head, suddenly feeling a sense of embarrassment. "It's really yum..." Genevieve offered me a kind smile, it was comforting, I lifted the cup to my lips and could feel a smile on route to my face, it was like nothing I had ever tasted before, it was like heaven.

WYNTER

"Wynter, pst…" Genevieve called me over, I felt uncomfortable leaving Violet but I made my way over to her and sat down "What's with your friend, is she like an alien or something?" I looked over to Violet who was stuffing Cheetos into her mouth a handful at a time.

"She's just, unique… " I shrugged, "She's homeschooled and her dad is kind of strict, I like her, she's different…"

"You always did attract the weirdos…"

"She's not weird, she's just quirky, I think we could all do with being a bit more like Violet…"
I stood up and bounded towards Violet who was now on her 4th cup of fruit punch.

"You should really slow down on the sugar; you're going to get a sugar rush…" I laughed, Violet wiped her pink moustache with the back of her hand, I took a fist full of m&m's in my hand. "Here catch!" I threw one towards Violet and it hit her on the forehead, we both erupted into laughter.

"You now!" Violet did the same and missed me completely.
We continued with our game, as if there was no one else there, like it was just us two, in our own little world, two outcasts, two best friends.

The remnants of the sugar-fuelled party were clinging to our fingertips as I walked Violet home, her cheeks flush with excitement, despite the purple bags under her tired eyes, Violet's spirit remained unbending. As we approached Violet's house, my heart began to swell with a mix of joy and bittersweetness. I knew the day couldn't last forever but I wanted it to so badly—our sugar high would fade, and reality would creep back in, but for now, in the quiet moment where we walked together down the narrow pavement without uttering a word to one another but being silently happy to be in one another's company, it was perfect. We rounded the corner to Violet's home and I thought about the memories weaving into the fabric of the weeks we'd shared together, but I could feel the nerves radiating from Violet's skin the closer we got. The streetlights flickered on, casting their warm glow, Violet's slumped silhouette moving in the light. I wondered what was on her mind, what troubled her, I wondered what secrets Violet bared inside of her head.

"How bad is it going to be?" I broke the silence, she shrugged, her fragile frame struggling to keep her up right and she turned to me.

"This was the best day ever..." She attempted a smile but I could sense the disappointment, a similar disappointment to the one that I had towards the day being over. I worried for Violet; I could go all day without my mother knowing I was gone but I hoped for her sake we have pulled off our plan. Out of the blue, Violet wrapped her arms around me, I could feel her jagged bones through her skin as she tightened her grip around my body.

"Oh, your dress!" I reached into my backpack as she let go and retrieved her dress, she took it in her hand before making her way up the path, causing the porch light to flicker on, she hugged the wall to the side of the house and switched dresses before waving to me as she retreated inside, I waited for a few moments before leaving.

The wind whispered secrets in my ears, as it tugged at my dress. I glanced up at the moon that had just suddenly appeared in the sky, a pale crescent hanging low. It seemed to watch over my every move, its silver glow both comforting and somewhat eerie. I wondered if the moon ever felt lonely up there, surrounded by endless darkness. As I passed the park, memories surfaced. Summers spent chasing fireflies with my sisters, lying on sun-warmed grass. Now, the swings hung frozen, their chains creaking in protest, like something from a horror movie I wasn't supposed to watch but did anyway. The old oak tree stood stationary near the corner, its gnarled branches reaching for the sky, as if pleading for warmth. I touched its rough bark, imagining it as a guardian— a silent witness to countless walks home. There it was— the familiar glow. My house, with its peeling paint and crooked mailbox. I could see my mother through the window, in the same position I left her passed out on the couch as per usual.

"Wynter!" A familiar voice interrupted my thoughts, I turned to see that is was Dominic. "It's getting late, what are you still doing out?" I wasn't used to adults questioning me and it did get my back up slightly.

"I'm just heading home…" I sighed, avoiding his eye contact, I didn't want him to know that although his relationship with my mother was short lived, I missed him, the way she was when we were around him, the way I felt.

"you must be freezing!" He noticed my thin dress and bare legs.

"It was warmer when I put this on…" I paused "What are you doing here anyways? I thought you and mama broke up?"

"We did, I was just in town, sometimes I run in this area"

"Oh…" I looked down with disappointment "She was happier when she was with you Dominic"

"Wynter, your mama is fighting some demons I just can't fix…"

"Can't or won't?"

"A bit of both" he admitted "You may understand when you're older Wynter…"

"don't tell me I don't understand, I understand…. More than you'd think…" Before I could stop them tears had begun cascading down my cheeks "I just wanted someone to take care of me, instead of me having to take

care of everyone else."
Dominic shuffled his feet, he was wearing running shorts and his legs had begun to goosepimple.

"Come on, let me walk you in…"
He put his arm around me and walked me inside, we crept past my mother to the bedroom where Alma and Cleo were playing with their dolls, they should have been in bed. He picked Cleo up; she had been clearly sitting in a soiled diaper all day as the stench was prominent.

"Where do you keep the diapers?" Dominic queried, I nodded towards a bag that sat in the corner of the room, he took the bag and Cleo to another room and when he returned she seemed smiley and giggly.

"How do you girls fancy a story?"

"Really?" I could feel my eyes lighting up, I had never felt like a kid before, but in that moment I felt warm and happy, I felt like how I imagined other kids in my class at school felt. I got into bed with Cleo on one side and Alma on the other and Dominic draped the blanket over us before kneeling on the hard floor beside the mattress. I still don't remember what the story was about, only how I felt in that moment and when I woke up the next morning, he was gone.

Early that Sunday morning, I waited for Violet to appear at the fence like she always did, I waited for hours, but she didn't come. I paced the path back and forth like a caged lion, worry embedded deep inside my brain. Maybe she was just sick, maybe her father grounded her for sneaking out. The first day I dismissed it, but as the sun dipped below the horizon each evening, leaving shadows in its wake, my concerns deepened. My brain running wild with scenarios. On the third day I braved it, approaching Violet's house, the curtains drawn and the lights out, the air smelled of neglect, a stale mix of unwashed dishes and alcohol, much like my own home. I hesitated before knocking, no one answered, maybe no one was home, could Violet and her father have just up and left? My mind spun tales of what might have happened my brain racing uncontrollably with thoughts, what if Violet was in trouble? I imagined myself as the heroin, the one who'd go in all guns blazing and save the day, the only problem was, I didn't even know if she needed to be saved. The fourth day brought rain, a relentless downpour that ran down the road like a vicious creek, drenching through my clothes, but still, I waited. At night I lay awake staring at the ceiling, imagining Violet, the freckles on each cheek that were joined with the freckles on her nose, the gap between her two front teeth when she smiled, if something had happened to her I'd never have forgiven myself. On the fifth day I sat where we always sat, making daisy chains, one for me, one for Violet, and that's when I saw it, a figure emerging from the shadows, it was Violet, dishevelled, her eyes wide like a deer in the headlights. Where had she been all this time and why did she look like she had been to hell and back?

"Violet..." I breathed a sigh of relief. "I was worried sick..."
Violet didn't sit, she remained standing, frozen to the spot as if someone had pressed pause on her, somehow she seemed more fragile than before. She was filthy, like she had just emerged from a fire and her eyes were dull and sad looking, her matted hair once just simply messy now resembled tangled vines.

"You can't come here anymore Wynter..."
"What? What do you mean?"
"He's always watching..."

Violet wrapped her fragile hands around the raw iron of the fence, she had dirt under her nails.

"Well can't we just go around the back?"
"I'm not supposed to come out here anymore, I'm taking a risk even coming out to see you, but since you wouldn't leave I had to come see you..."
"Violet, what happened?"
Violet sighed.
"you're the only friend I've ever had Wynter, I

don't get to see people much, I stay inside the house most of the day, seeing you is the best part of my day, if it wasn't for you, my bubble would be really small, I wouldn't smile as much and I wouldn't know as much, you didn't just teach me about words and numbers, you taught me how to be me..."

"Alright, well please, please don't just throw this away, I need you, more than you know"
Violet fell to her knees.

"I feel weak Wynter..."

"Maybe you're coming down with something..." I touched my hand to her forehead, it was hot like flames and her skin was clammy, like when Alma got the flu that one time. "I can get you some medicine tomorrow, I'll bring it to you after school, okay?"

"I told you; I can't come out..."

"Then I'll come in... You need medicine Violet, you're burning up..."

The next day, the second the bell rang for the end of school I was out of there. I raced from my school to Alma's to pick her up then to the childminders to get Cleo before making my way with Cleo on my hip and Alma attached to my hand to the chemist that sat 2 miles outside of Sherwood.

"Wynnie, slow down, I'm shorter than you!" Alma called as I dragged her down the street. As I pushed the heavy door of the chemist open, I clutched the crumpled 5-dollar bill that I had borrowed from my mother's purse. The pharmacist, a kind faced woman with glasses perched on the end of her nose, looked up from her paperwork.

"Hello dear," She said "How can I help you today?"

"It's for my mama" I lied, "She's not feeling well, so I said I'd pick her up some medicine..." My voice wavered, lying had become like second nature to me but still my heart raced.

"What are her symptoms?"

"Weak with a fever..."
The pharmacist came out from behind her desk and headed to the back of the store, I followed her blindly with my sisters. Alma leaned in close to me.
"Is mama really sick?"
"No, I'll explain later..." I whispered through gritted teeth.
We all drew to a halt, the pharmacist reached to the top shelf and brought down a small bottle filled with liquid and lead us back to the front desk, I couldn't even attempt to read what was on the label.
"What is it?" I asked
"This stuff is like gold dust; she should feel better after a day or so... That'll be 5.98"
"This is all I have..." I handed her the five-dollar bill.
"Oh did I say 5.98, I meant 5 dollars..." The pharmacist winked at me, I offered her a warm relieved smile, grabbed the medicine and we left. I took Alma and Cleo home first before bolting at top speed to Violet's house. All of a sudden fear struck me down like lightening and I was stopped in my tracks on the wrong side of the fence. I didn't know what to expect inside that house but even though fear had a choke hold on me, I took three breaths before squeezing my slender body through the gap in the fence and darting towards the house. I looked through the window, the curtains were drawn but there was a slight gap that I could see through, I could see Violet's father, sitting on the couch, beer in hand, not unlike my own mother, perhaps Violet and I were more alike than I had first thought. I ducked as he turned his attention towards the window, hearing him get up to look out, I lay myself down on the ground, close to the building, when I was sure he was gone, I rose to my feet again. Staying close to the building I moved around to the door, trying the handle, it was open, as I pushed it, it creaked, I paused in my tracks but when no one came I knew it was safe to enter. Now, to find Violet, I looked around, the

décor was outdated and there wasn't a single-family picture hanging on the wall. There was a door almost immediately next to the front door, slowly I opened it, there was stairs that led down to a room that was almost entirely pitch black, aside from a dim light that barely lit up a corner of the room. Something told my feet to follow the light, so they did. At the back of the room, on a camp bed, lay Violet, she was either sleeping or dead, I hoped sleeping.

"Violet..." She stirred, phew, she was just sleeping. "I brought you some medicine, it should help..." Violet turned her head to face me, her cheeks flushed and her eyes glassy. I pulled the medicine bottle from my pocket, suddenly realising I didn't have a spoon but I did have the idea to use the lid of the bottle. It cracked as I opened it before I poured a capful of the liquid, it was thick and sticky.

"You have to sit up to take this..."

She struggled to sit up, her arms trembling, I poured the medicine directly into her mouth, she gagged and choked at the taste before swallowing hard. I screwed the cap back on and placed the bottle on the floor, I brushed her hair that was sticking to her wet forehead to the side and helped her lie back down.

"How did you get in here?"

"I have my ways" I laughed

"I told you it wasn't safe..."

"Does your dad know you're sick?"

"My father doesn't really believe in medicine, he says if you are tough you should be able to fight it on your own..."

I looked around, the room where Violet slept seemed cold, in temperature and in décor, the walls were bare and stone, the floor was uncarpeted and she didn't appear to have very many belongings.

"You sleep down here?"

The stale scent of dampness enveloped my nostrils, dusty shelves, although empty seemed to bear the weight of a thousand secrets, water dripped from the ceiling and echoed in a cruel slow torture and cobwebs hung on every corner, this wasn't a bedroom, this was more like a prison.

"Yeah…" Violet coughed violently.

The cold seeped into my bones, I could only imagine how she felt it on her slight, breakable frame. My ears perked up to the sound of footsteps coming from above and panic set in. Violets eyes widened.

"Lift the rug, there's a door under there, you can hide in there until it's safe to come out…" Violet whispered, after grabbing the medicine bottle and forcing it into my pocket I did just that. Suddenly I put two and two together, this was where Violet was that time I snuck into the garden. The footsteps became more crisp and clearer.

"you look rough." A husky male voice that I assumed to be Violet's father spoke.

"I'm okay…" Violet lied.

The concrete hole that I had suddenly found myself in seemed to swallow all light, the walls were rough and unyielding, I stood with my back pressed against the textured wall, my breath misting as I breathed out into the chilled air. I felt small and insignificant, like a speck of dust on a windowsill.

"Have you learned your lesson?"

"Yes"

"The rules are for your own good Violet; you know that don't you?"

"I know…"

"Good girl…"

The voices ceased and it fell quiet. I held my breath for what seemed like an eternity.

"Wynter, it's safe"

I climbed up the slippery ladders and emerged through the door, closing it quietly behind me and placing the rug back over it.

"What even is that in there?"

Violet didn't answer, instead she just pursed her lips, I could tell she was uneasy, so I changed the subject.

"I brought some stuff, I thought we could do some reading" I pulled to kill a mocking bird out of my bag "I think you're ready" I handed her the book, she ran the palm of her hand down the front cover as if to see if it was real and her face lit up as she opened to the first page.

"When he was nearly thirteen my brother Jem got his arm badly broken at the… What does that word say?"

"Elbow"

"Right… Elbow…. When he was nearly thirteen my brother Jem got his arm badly broken at the elbow."

I walked home that night feeling lighter but also confused by the enigma that was Violet… As I approached my house, I saw an unfamiliar red car parked outside and on approach to the front door I could see my mother with another woman, a smaller woman, my mother was flailing her arms around angrily and when I entered the house I found out why.

"You must be Wynter, my name is Stephanie Myers from social services…."

PEYTON

My self and Lara were called into a meeting with Principal Holden, or Agatha as we knew her, first thing in the morning, I had barely even taken my coat off.

"late last night, social services were called to the home of Wynter Jones"

"Wait, what happened?"

"Apparently Wynter's baby sister was left crying for hours whilst her mother was passed out on the couch…"

"wait, mother? Wynter told me her mother was dead…"

"I can assure you Peyton, Wynter Jones's mother is very much alive…" Why would she lie about that? I wondered. "After some discussion, it was agreed that social services would work with her to get sober, they'll be checking up on her weekly, the kids remain in her care, for the time being, she is apparently pregnant with a fourth child but it's just to make you aware…"

My hands trembled as I made my way back to my class and anxiously awaited the arrival of my string of students. When the bell rang for them to arrive in class, there was one very noticeably missing. I glanced at the clock—the seconds ticking like a countdown. The students chattered, oblivious to the weight of the moment. My gaze fell on the empty seat, plagued with worry I couldn't bring myself to begin the class. Wynter was my star pupil, the most intelligent child I had yet met and I worried that fact weighed heavy on her much like other parts of her life that she kept to herself and just got on with it. The lesson was, suffering wasn't always obvious, it wasn't always bubbling by the surface, Wynter was screaming but no one was hearing. Seconds turned to minutes and Wynter still hadn't arrived but just when I had given up hope, the classroom door squealed open.

"Sorry I'm late Miss, I slept in…" She looked drained, her once vibrant eyes seemed to now hold a dull weariness, the dark circles beneath her eyes told a silent tale of many sleepless nights, her shoulders slumped bearing the burden of responsibilities far beyond the realms of an 11-year-old, she dragged her school bag behind her like a ball and chain of all her woes. She sat down, her eyes fixated on the window, but today, I let her escape into her own world because I knew that is what she needed.

After class I had asked Wynter to wait behind, as the rest of the children filtered out the door she stayed put at her desk, her eyes heavy, in her own world. I made my way over to where she was sitting.
"Wynter..."
Wynter looked up towards where I was standing, her voice mumbling an apology for not finishing her homework, comfortingly I rested my hand on her shoulder, I felt her quiver beneath my fingertips as if she wanted to break down but couldn't.
"I'm sorry I lied to you about my mama...."
"It's okay... I understand..."
"I feel like an awful person, I love my mama, she just, needs help..."
"Wynter, listen to me okay? I just want you to know, if you ever need to talk, about anything at all, I'll always be here to listen..."
"I'm scared Miss Larkin..."
Wynter allowed herself to be vulnerable for just a moment as I wrapped her up in my arms, my heart ached for her.
"It's okay..." I whispered.
I wished I could take her pain away; she looked up to me with swollen eyes and tear-stained cheeks.
"How do you know?"
"I don't, but it has to be, nothing stays bad forever..."
She allowed herself to smile, the dimples on her cheeks prominent and deep. We sat in silence for several moments, I wondered if she felt the comfort like I did, the connection, the girl that once was an enigma to me, I was

beginning to understand better.

"Thank you Miss Larkin…." She broke the silence, her voice soft and wavering. I wiped the tears from her cheeks with my thumb. I knew what it was like to feel pain so deep that it genuinely felt like you may die of a broken heart, I remembered the moment I was told of my husband's passing, every feeling came flooding back to me.

"You're welcome…" I snapped back to earth. Wynter filed her books into her backpack, slung one strap over her shoulder and walked out without looking back.

I could hear Penny crying from the next room, the sort of cry that came out of frustration as opposed to a skint knee or a bumped head. When I entered her room she was red with rage, pulling at her barbie doll whose hair had become entrapped in the hinge of her doll house. I knelt down next to her, gently taking the barbie from her hand and releasing her from the doll house's grasp. I handed her the doll and scooped her up into my arms.

"I know it feels like the end of the world but I promise you it isn't" I cradled her head in my hands, I imagined what life would have been like if her father had been here to watch her grow. What kind of father would he have been, would he have been tough and strict? Would he have been gentle and kind? Would he have been goofy? Or all of the above.

"Mama…" She wrapped her chubby fingers around my thumb. "Penny have ice cream?"
Penny hadn't been stringing sentences together for long so when she did it made me beam with pride.

"Alright, since you asked so nicely"
I lifted her through to the kitchen, sat her on the counter and retrieved a small vanilla ice pop from the freezer. Penny beamed with pride as she demolished it getting it all over her face and hands, but that was the beauty of having a toddler. I looked up at the time, 7PM, maybe It wasn't the best idea to give my two-year-old ice-cream

right before bed, but I was a single mother and sometimes I just wanted to be good cop.

As I sat on the edge of my daughters "big girl" bed, stroking her hair I thought about how lucky she was, I thought about Wynter and the hardships she faced on the daily and I hoped that I could shield Penny from those types of hardships. I knew I couldn't but I'd try anyway. She had her father's hazel eyes and when they were sleepy it was even more prominent.

"I wuv you mama..." She spoke softly, as she gripped the stuffed lamb that she had since she was born. It was a gift from my sister.

"I love you too baby..." I kissed her forehead gently "Now, get some sleep..."

"Are the monsters in the closet gone?"

"Yes sweetie, mama got them with the vacuum" Penny smiled sweetly before slowly closing her eyes and rolling onto her side, I watched for a moment from the door before closing it slightly, leaving it open a crack so the light from the hall left a trail of golden light in her room. Penny was afraid of the dark like most children were, I remember it from my own childhood, being afraid of what may come out of the darkness, the fear of the unknown.

Not long after putting Penny to bed, I tucked myself up in bed. On my bedside cabinet sat a picture of my wedding day, I remembered it well, the best day of my life besides the birth of our daughter. I felt like a princess that day.

"I love you Bailey" I whispered to the picture "More than you'd ever know. I blew my husband a kiss and drifted off to sleep.

VIOLET

It only took me a few days to start feeling better after taking the medicine Wynter had brought me, I took it twice a day in secret and hid it beneath my bed far away from my father's prying eyes. Things got bad after Wynter had helped me sneak out, my father had come home early to check on me and when he realised I wasn't there, it wasn't pretty, let's just say it consisted of many days in confinement, no food, no water and chilling to the bone, he had disciplined me, I could still see the fire iron when I closed my eyes, but I deserved it, I was defiant, just like he said, I was ungrateful and useless and didn't show him that I appreciated him for everything he had done for me, taking me in when no one else wanted me, but Wynter was my best friend, my only friend so I was torn in two like two sides of coin, one side was my father, my shelter, he who giveth and he who taketh away and on the other side was Wynter, my life line, my guardian angel who had rescued me when things were grey.

"Violet, I am heading out to work...."
The words I was dreading, I knew what that meant, my father had begun a new discipline method to stop me from sneaking out until he could trust me again. He came bounding down the stairs, he seemed in a good mood today, maybe he wouldn't... My thoughts were interrupted when I saw it. He had fashioned the rope with a tight knot making a loop, he placed it around my ankle and pulled the dangling piece of rope to tighten it until it felt like it would force its way through my skin to the bone, he fastened the other side of the rope to a loop of iron he had attached to the wall tightly so that I could only move a few steps in each direction but it wasn't even worth it due to the agony it caused.

"Be good alright?" My father placed his massive, rough hands on either side of my face, his face so close to mine I could practically taste what he had for breakfast.

"I will..."
He kissed my forehead before heading off to work. Moments after I was sure he was gone, I called her out.
"Wynter, it's all clear..."
Wynter had snuck in first thing in the morning after her sisters had headed out with their fathers. She emerged from the trap door in the floor.
"It stinks down there..."
"I know, it's freezing cold too"
"I brought breakfast"
Wynter dipped her hand into her bag, as she did I hid my leg below myself so that she couldn't see the rope, I didn't want to have to explain it. Wynter pulled out two bananas that were speckled with brown spots, she handed me one along with a carton of apple juice.
"It's not much but it's all we have at home at the minute, but the social worker is going to make us a care package this week so hopefully it'll be better..."
"What's a social worker?"
Wynter gulped hard, her eyes dropping to the ground, for some reason my question seemed to make her sad. It was a simple question in my mind, yet it seemed to carry the weight of a thousand unspoken fears. Wynter hesitated, her hands clasped on her lap.
"It's complicated Violet" She finally sighed.
Wynter's gaze shifted to the small, barred window high above. If only she knew that she could trust me as I trusted her, if only she knew that I could be there for her like she was for me.
"Wynter..." I reached for her hand and took it in my own, it was cold, much like her demeanour. "you don't always have to keep it all in..."
She took a deep breath, her own vulnerability laid bare.
"A social worker," Wynter began softly, "A social worker is someone who helps people..."
"Helps them with what?"
"Well, it depends..."
"What do you have one for?"

"My mama needs some help to, well, be a mama, it's not her fault, she's sick"
"Like I was sick?"
"Sort of... There's different kinds of sick...."
I wasn't following, but before I could ask further questions Wynter had changed the subject.
"I brought games!" She reached into her bag again and pulled out two dusty boxes. "Uno, or connect 4?"

Wynter stayed with me for the entire day, we played games, laughed, talked and read to kill a mockingbird together. I was getting really good at reading and Wynter had taught me how to write my own name. Our fun was interrupted by the slam of the front door upstairs.
"Quick, hide!" I whispered through gritted teeth, panic setting in my bones. I stood up to help Wynter tidy up her things into her bag.
"What's that on your ankle?"
I had gone all day without her noticing and had fallen at the last hurdle.
"It's a long story, Wynter, you've got to hide, quick!"
I could hear the door to the basement screech open and the footsteps echoing down the stairs, Wynter hurriedly moved the rug and entered the hole to confinement, I closed it behind her and placed the rug back where it belonged and sat back down on my bed just in the nick of time, panting with a mixture of dread and anxiety. My father appeared out of the shadows, wearing his work uniform.
"nice to see you're becoming more obedient Violet..."
I nodded as he crouched down, knife in hand, to cut the rope from my ankle. The moment the rope was cut, relief flooded through my pulsing veins, The sensation was both painful and liberating though my skin bore the imprint of

its twisted fibres and throbbed but the pain was welcome as it reminded me that I was still alive and breathing.

"Thank you father…" I rubbed my ankle where the rope had been, my fingers tracing the indents.

"I don't like punishing you like this Violet, but it's for your own good, you know that right?"

"Father," I gulped, nerves tingling throughout my body "can you tell me what my family was like?"
Oh no, I could feel the rage rising from his feet right through to his head, I wished I could just swallow my words and stop them from pushing their way out of my mouth.

"You ungrateful little brat! Have you learned nothing? They didn't want you! I took you in, gave you a home, gave you everything you'd ever need and still it's not enough!"
My father struck me in the face with the back of the hand, the impact stinging my cheek and knocking me onto the cold concrete floor, he stood up towering over me.

"I wasn't trying to be ungrateful father, I'm sorry"
My father lifted his foot, bearing a steel toe capped boot and pressed it down onto my ankle so fiercely I thought my whole foot would just snap off. I grunted in anguish, feeling the tears welling up in my eyes but attempting to hold them back, he pressed down harder again before releasing and stepping back, without saying another word he retreated back up the stairs slamming the door. I felt like a shell of a human, broken, worthless. Wynter sprung from the hole to my aid, she knelt down next to me.

"Violet, this isn't normal, you know that right?"
Part of me did know that, but the other part of me just longed to be loved. Wynter placed a gentle hand on my back.

"He just cares about me…"

"That's not caring, look, it's swelling"

"I'll be fine, I'll just walk it off"
I rose to my feet but my ankle buckled and I fell back down.

"Does he do this often?"

"Only when I'm bad…"

My ankle had already began to bruise and was turning purple.

"Here, I got you a present, I wasn't going to give you it yet, but I think you need it…"

Wynter handed me a purple box from the front pocket of her bag, the box was sealed with a silk bow. I slowly untied the bow and lifted the lid on the box, inside was the most beautiful thing I had ever seen. A silver chain with a pendant at the end of it, the pendant was half a heart and said the word, B for Books, E for Elephant, S for snake and T for Trike, "BEST".

"Here…" Wynter took the necklace from me and put it around my neck, clicking it at the back, I held it in my hands, it felt so fragile yet stood for so much. "I have one too…" Wynter took her pendant out from under her shirt. "Mine says friends, like best friends." Wynter held up her half heart, as did I and we fit them together, they fit together just like she and I had.

"Wynter, it's so beautiful, thank you"

I pulled her into a warm tight embrace, suddenly the weight of the world felt so much lighter because I knew that we were in it together.

After Wynter left I lay in bed, holding my pendant in my hand, thinking about all the memories from the moment I met her until now, I wondered what the future held, we had already faced so much together and she had taught me so much, our times together were the only thing keeping me going.

WYNTER

Every Thursday at 4:30, Stephanie from social services would visit us at home. Before it my mother and I would run around like two headless chickens fixing up the house and making sure everything was in order. I'd dress Cleo and Alma in their best clothes and do their hair to make them look presentable whilst my mother would go around with a bin bag picking rubbish up off the floor and mopping the kitchen floor.

"Why do I need to wear this stupid bow?" Alma squirmed as I tightened the red silk bow in her pigtails. "It's babyish"

"As soon as the social worker is gone, you can take it out."

There was a knock at the door, my mother breathed in so deep, I thought she would swallow us all whole.

"Good morning Mrs Jones" Stephanie chirped as my mother opened the door. Stephanie was short in stature, she was heavier set with hazelnut brown hair scraped into a bun at the top of her head with horn-rimmed glasses that covered her chestnut brown eyes, she couldn't have been much older and 30 but she dressed like a woman in her 80's and smelled like stale perfume. My mother invited her to sit down in the living room. Her arrival felt like a sudden gust of wind, the atmosphere was grey and meek. When she had stepped over the threshold of the door, her shoes left a faint imprint on our worn-out carpet. Her eyes darted around the room, taking it all in, I wasn't sure what she was looking for but although my mother wasn't perfect, I hated how this stranger was invading our space. Her gaze lingered on the cracked window, the faded curtains, and the single, dim light bulb hanging from the ceiling, I prayed she wouldn't notice the cobwebs in the corner of every room.

"How have things been?" Stephanie spoke with a

soft yet authoritative voice.

"They've been great, haven't had a drop of alcohol since your last visit."

That was a lie, just the night before I had found her passed out on the grass at the front of the house and had to virtually drag her back inside but still, I smiled and nodded when my mother spoke.

"That's great... I was hoping for the opportunity to speak to both Alma and Wynter individually?"

My mother had coached us, we were to say how our mother was out every day handing out CV's looking for work, she wasn't, we were to tell her how she'd been sober and how we'd spent a lot of family time together, we hadn't and lastly we were to smile and be polite. Stephanie spoke to me first, in the living room, whilst my mother waited with Alma and Cleo in the bedroom.

"tell me Wynter, on a scale from 1 to 10, how would you rate your home life at the minute..."

About a 4, the only saving graces being Alma and Cleo and of course my honorary sister Violet.

"About an 8..." I lied, smiling just like mama told me to, so much so that my cheeks started to burn.

"Good, that's great, your mama says you're doing more together now, what kind of things are you doing?"

"We uh..." I paused to think "we have movie nights, yeah, mama gets snacks in and we all snuggle on the couch and watch movies..."

I wished that we had nights like that, my whole life that was all I ever wanted but at that moment all I could think about was, did I sound convincing enough? I studied Stephanie - the lines etched on her face; the pen tucked behind her ear. I wondered if she could see beyond the peeling wallpaper, beyond the secrets hidden within the four white walls. She asked more questions about school, about friends about my sisters, she wanted to know what I was eating, did I have someone to go to when I needed it, with every question it felt like the walls were closing in, like she was encroaching into the inside of my brain.

"Wynter, is everything okay?" She interrupted my thoughts and brought me crashing back to earth.

"Yes, are we done here...?"

"Yes we are, thank you for speaking with me Wynter..."

I smiled just like my mother told me to and retreated to my room.

Not long after Stephanie left my mother opened a beer and sprawled out on the sofa, her baby bump had started to show slightly but that didn't stop her from her drinking and smoking, I tucked Alma and Cleo under the blanket, Cleo was being fussy but relaxed when I gave her the milk I had prepared for her.

"Who is that lady Wynnie?" Alma perked up; an innocent curiosity written all over her face. "She's really nosy!"

"She's a social worker"

"She asks a lot of questions..."

I laughed, tucking a strand of hair behind her ear.

"She does, but she just wants to make sure we are okay, that's we're cared for..."

"You take real good care of us Wynter..."

I let myself smile, cradling Alma's little hand in my own, all I had ever wanted was for my sisters to be happy, for their lives to be easy, even if that meant mine had to be hard, I wanted it for them.

"Alright, sleep tight okay? Don't let the bed bugs bite."

I kissed Alma's head and then I kissed Cleo's head, she reached up and placed a hand on both of my cheeks.

"Mama" She spoke, clear as day, her first word, I wasn't her mother, but most days I felt like I was, I pulled the blanket up to her chin and stroked the soft fine hair on the top of her head with my hand.

"Good night Cleo..."

I left the house just after 10PM, after I was sure the whole house was out for the night.
"Wynter! It's late, where are you going?"
Dominic called, he was doing his usual late-night run, but I was sure there was more to it, was he spying on us? If so, why?
"Are you following me?"
"No, I told you, this is where I run!"
"Like you said Dominic, it's late…"
Dominic sighed, like he had something to get off his chest.
"Do you like tea Wynter"
I nodded and we walked the 15-minute walk to Dominic's house, he lived at the end of a dirt road track, in a little red bungalow, the first thing I thought of when I saw it was the life we could have had if my mother had stayed with Dominic. The peeling paint on the wooden exterior of his house revealed layers of history, I wondered if he had inherited it from an elderly relative or bought it from someone else, adding to their story. Moonlight filtered through the overgrown trees, casting dappled shadows on the porch which held a swing it was weathered and creaking, swaying gently in the breeze, if this was a horror movie, I'd have been screaming at the protagonist to run the other way, but I felt safe with Dominic.
"You can leave your shoes on… I ain't precious" He said as we stepped into his home, my breath caught my throat as I inhaled the scent of old wood, dampness and paint, A faded runner rug led deeper into the house, its colours muted with the amount of feet that must have trampled over it, that must be where the phrase don't let people walk all over you came from. Dominic led me into the living room, it was simply lit, red Threadbare curtains hung at the windows, filtering the moonlight into soft rectangles. A worn-out sofa sagged in the corner, its floral pattern barely recognisable. I imagined myself Alma and Cleo sitting there, being warmed by the fireplace that sat adjacent, if things has gone differently. Dominic motioned for me to sit down.

"What do you take in your tea?"
"Tea?"
"Yeah, you said you liked tea..."
I had no idea why I said that, I'd never had tea before.
"Um..."
"I have juice too..."
"Juice will be fine please..."
Dominic smirked out the corner of his mouth and retreated to what I assumed was the kitchen. I looked to the fireplace where pictures sat idly, moments frozen in time. My gaze lingered on one picture in particular, it was a picture of a young girl my age and one slightly younger, the older one had Dominic's face.
"I didn't know you had kids..." I observed as Dominic handed me my juice and sat down with his tea on the chair in front of me.
"Yeah, they're my two, Sophie, she's your age and Matilda, she's 7, I share custody with my ex-wife, but God it's hard when it's her turn to have em"
Dominic gingerly brought his piping hot steaming tea to his lips and took a sip without even flinching.
"how come you broke up with..."
"My ex-wife?" He interrupted "I didn't, she broke it off with me, for another guy, younger, richer, same old story..."
"I'm sorry Dominic..."
"Don't be, it was a while ago now, we separated when my youngest was 3..."
The air fell silent, I knew he had brought me here for a reason but I didn't dare ask why but I noticed his fingers tracing the rim of his mug nervously.
"Why'd you bring me here Dominic?" I finally asked.
He sat back in his chair, placing his mug on the side table and sighed, like he had let out all the air he held inside his body.
"I care about you Wynter, and despite everything I still care about your mother too..."

"I know…"
"She's pregnant Dominic…"
"I know…"
"I can't look after another kid, I just can't…"
"I know Wynter, and everything I did, I did because I want your mother to get better, and you and your sisters to have a better life, and the new baby okay?" My interest was piqued, I sat forward on the couch, leaning towards him, my heart beating through my chest.
"What did you do?"
"I was the one who called the social worker"
All of a sudden a bubbling and burning sensation slowly began to rise, starting at my feet and travelling North. Dominic was clasping his hands so hard his knuckles began to turn pale white.
"You did what?!?" I rose to my feet abruptly.
"I'm sorry Wynter, but it's no way to live, your mother, she needs help, your sisters need more care than you can give them"
"You don't know what my sisters need!" My voice was croaky from shrieking "I will never forgive you for this!"
Without a second thought I was out of there, not looking back, my blood boiling, my heart racing, my body shaking, It was cold outside but I was so furious that I didn't even notice.

I didn't go home right away, I went to the only place where I felt like my life wasn't falling apart, Violet's, I was pretty sure in the "sucky" life race, she won hands down. Since her father caught her sneaking back in from the party, he had really tightened the strings. He kept her secured by the ankle to the wall in her basement bedroom. It was freezing down there and she was only wearing a thin dress but for some reason it didn't bother her too much. I wondered if she was happy or if she sometimes wished for a different life. I wondered if a social worker showed up randomly to her house, would she be pleased or would she be as mad as I was?

"Wynter, you seem sad today..."

Since knowing Violet she had learned to become more and more socially and emotionally aware, I both loved and hated it.

"It's just been a tough day..."

"Is this about the social worker?"

It was and it wasn't, it was about Dominic going behind my back and trying to be the hero, it was about my mother continuing to drink herself into an early grave all the while acting the angel in front of the social worker, it was about the social worker poking her nose in where it didn't belong, it was about my mother being pregnant and acting like it wasn't the end of the world and it was about how it all weighed so heavy on my shoulders I felt like I could barely stand up. I didn't answer Violet but I could tell she understood, my silence was deafening.

"My father got me some paper and pencils to keep my mind off trouble, do you want to draw with me?"

I nodded as she handed me a blank piece of white paper and scattered the pencils on the floor, as she did, she reached for my hand and took it in hers, her face full of sorrow, I didn't let myself break down, but when I got home that night I cried myself to sleep.

PEYTON

In the weeks following my encounter with Wynter Jones, she seemed different, distracted even, she spent most of the lessons looking out of the window, the far-off stare of someone who had the weight of the world crushing them. At recess I could see her from my classroom, sitting under the old oak tree at the back of the school grounds, her nose in a book, she didn't talk to anyone, didn't seem to have any friends, and if she did, she was actively pushing them away.

"Is everything okay Wynter?" She nodded but her eyes were heavy and she was even more unkempt than usual. "You know, you can talk to me about anything…"

"I know… And when I have anything to talk about, I will…"

Wynter lumped all of her books into her back pack, the same back pack that was now missing a strap, was filled with holes and was caked in dirt, she slung it over her shoulder, shot me a smile, said "bye Miss Larkin" and walked out the door. I knew everything wasn't alright though, but there was only so much that I could do as a teacher, I wanted to scoop her up and hold her whilst she cried, take away all of her pain and fix any of her woes but I couldn't. I sat down in my chair, sinking so far into it that it seemed I would disappear.

"Did someone say Margaretas?" I felt myself being spun around in my chair, Lara had changed out of her usual pencil skirt and frilly blouse into something a little bit, tighter, a sparkly red, body-hugging number with black knee-high boots. "Are you coming out tonight?"

I hadn't planned on it; Penny was with the babysitter and I hadn't brought a change of clothes.

"I don't think so…"

"C'mon Pey, it'll be fun, you look like you could use a night out…"

She wasn't lying, I could use a night out, but did I want

one? That was another question.
"I can't go dressed like this"
"you look fine, like a million dollars"
I knew she was lying but I appreciated it.
"Okay, fine"
"Yeehaw!"

The main faculty hang out was a bar at the very back of Sherwood, "The Black Heart", it was a little grimy, a little bit divey, but it was a place we could guarantee not bumping into students, or their parents.
"What can I do ya for?" The waitress was wearing a black sparky body suit with a red bow tie around her neck, fish net tights and heels that I definitely couldn't walk in, I ordered a white wine.
"Pey, you're killin me here, could you at least pretend you are havin fun?"
"Sorry, it's just not really my scene..."
That wasn't all, it had been a rough week, I'd been losing sleep both because my toddler was fussy but also because of Wynter, I had become a little bit too invested in her story, so much more than my remit but I did worry about my students, we weren't supposed to get to attached, just do our jobs, prepare them for the big bad world and send them on their way but I couldn't help it.
"Come on, take a shot with me!" Lara slid two lime green coloured shots over to where we were sitting at the end of a long table of our colleagues. She counted to three and then we both knocked it back; it burned but Lara didn't even flinch. "Okay, what's bothering you...?"
"I just worry about her..."
"Who?"
"Wynter Jones, what if she ends up like that Bees kid, you know, the one the art room was named after.."
"That was completely different Peyton"
"How?"
"It just is..."
"We don't know what happens behind closed

doors…"

"Social work are handling it, there is nothing more you can do…"

"I wish there was…"

"Pey, you can't save everyone, you know?"
She was right, I knew she was right but I wished she was wrong.

"I wish I could…"
Lara placed her hand comfortingly on my leg.

"C'mon, let's dance." She whispered in my ear, her breath smelling like the shot we had just consumed.
I hated dancing, I hated clubs, I hated loud music, I would have much rather spent the night sitting on my couch with my daughter watching reruns of Dora the explorer but I was here, and I was going to have fun even if it killed me. I downed another shot, wiped the remnants of alcohol off of my chin and allowed Lara to drag me to the dance floor. At first, we were the only ones on there but it soon filled up.

It wasn't long before I could barely hold myself up and Lara wasn't much better. My legs had taken on a life of their own. They pirouetted and stumbled, weaving a tipsy waltz across the sticky floor, Lara grabbed my arm to steady herself. Lara was a happy drunk, giggling, running around like an infant in the playground. Romi Hughes, the grade two teacher, she was a wild drunk, dancing on tables, downing shot after shot like it was the first time she had been let out. Jack Oliver, the pre-K teacher was a soppy drunk. "Has anyone ever told you, you have very pretty eyes?", "I just love you Peyton," "You look much more beautiful when you smile." It was both endearing and irritating. Sarah Darling, the lead office admin was an "I don't get drunk" drunk, no matter how much she drank, it didn't seem to affect her. Me? I was a more, philosophical drunk, "Why are trees green?" "What is the meaning of life?" That kind of thing.

"I told you if you just let your hair down you

might actually have fun..." Lara said as we slumped back down at our seats.

"Nobody likes a know it all....."

"I'll have a whiskey on the rocks" A voice distracted me from my thoughts. A woman at the bar, I recognized her, she had a slim build, so slim that her collar bone poked out aggressively, but she had a small baby bump sticking out when she turned to the side, her hair was dark, chest nut brown and slicked back into a ballet bun at the back of her head, she was wearing too much makeup and a black boob tube, jeans and silver stilettos.

"I haven't seen you around here before" The barman told her, his tongue practically hanging out and drooling.

"It's not my usual hangout, got banned from there..."

"A troublemaker huh?"

"You know it, I'm Lyric, Lyric Jones..." Lyric Jones? I'd know that name anywhere, there weren't many people in town called Lyric but I did know one, Wynter's mother, I remember seeing her name on the file when I was compiling information for the social worker. The thing about being drunk is, you can't always control your impulses, and with that, my feet started walking, I heard Lara audibly gasp as I walked off.

"Miss Jones..."

"Can I help you?"

"I'm your daughter teacher, Miss Larkin..."

"So...?"

"Do you really think it's a good idea to be out here drinking with what's going on at home, where are your kids? Plus you're pregnant..."

"I don't believe that is any of your business..." The barman handed Lyric her drink and she knocked it back like she had experience.

"Pey, not now, now here, come on..." Lara grabbed my arm and dragged me back to the table. I knew then that I had made a huge mistake, a mistake that very well may cost me my job.

$\mathcal{VIOLET}$

    The night was particularly stormy, the wind murmured outside my confines of the stony basement walls, worming its way through the cracks in the foundation caressing my cheeks and chilling me through to the bone. My father more often than not worked the nightshift now, he had gotten a new job, he wouldn't tell me what it was, all I knew was, it was terrifying being home alone at night. The door to my basement bedroom swung open, trembling I ran to the farthest corner of the room to coward in the corner.

    "Sorry Violet, I didn't mean to scare you..." Her silhouette became clearer after a few moments as she emerged from the darkness. It was Wynter and in her arms she held her younger sister Cleo and by her side, was Alma. "Sorry, she just really wanted to see you again..." I stood up from the corner I had placed myself in and Alma came bounding up to me wrapping her little arms around me in the tightest embrace in the world.

    "You don't have that thing on your ankle..." Wynter noticed as she descended the staircase.
My father didn't always remember to put the rope on, tonight was one of those nights, it was like a tiny moment of freedom.

    "Is this where you live Violet?" Alma questioned, looking around, her face telling of a thousand emotions she was feeling "It's, it's worse than our home..."

    "Alma, don't be rude!" Wynter elbowed Alma gently.

    "No, it's fine... This is just where I sleep Alma..."

    "Can we see the rest of the house?"
I thought for a moment before nodding,

    "Violet, are you sure?" Wynter spoke quietly,

through gritted teeth, the concern written all over her face. I nodded again before leading the way. I showed them the kitchen first, there were padlocks on all the doors, it was to stop me from sneaking food, Alma asked why they were there, I just told her the cupboards were broken and it was to keep them on, but I could tell Wynter knew the truth. Next we went to the area where my father watched TV with his big bowl of Cheetos. I had never watched TV but my father watched it a lot, he also ate a lot of Cheetos.

"Your dad ain't big on family pictures either huh? Our Mama never puts any up…"

"There is one picture." I reached over the back of the couch and pulled a framed picture from the shelf and handed it over to Wynter. "I'm not sure what age I was there, but I was pretty young…"

In the picture, I was smiling, standing on the grass, posing with my arms behind my back, my dress was a vibrant purple colour with ruffles on the sleeves and by the bottom, by my feet was a tattered teddy bear, it had one eye missing and looked like it had been through the wars, it had a name stitched to its arm which I assumed was my own but it was too small to really see, I looked so happy, I didn't even recognise the girl in the picture, she didn't seem like me at all. Wynter held it in one hand, Cleo on her hip, examining it, a smile creeped onto her face.

"You were so cute!"

She handed the picture back to me and I placed it back where I got it. As I did, Cleo reached her arms out to me and grabbed a hold of my dress.

"She wants you to hold her…" Alma whispered. Wynter nodded to me reassuringly, I had never been around a baby before. I had paid attention to how Wynter was holding her and tried to replicate it. She was warm and smelled of milk.

"Cleo hates everyone who isn't us, she must think you're pretty special Violet…"

We spent the next few hours playing scrabble, Wynter had taught me how to play and since I could spell some words now I found it to be pretty easy. It felt like I was their honorary sister, Cleo sat on my knee the entire time, her head burrowed into me, Alma sat stuck to me like glue, and Wynter took care of us all, like a mother.

"Do you remember anything about your birth mama Violet?" Alma perked up.

"Alma!"

"No, Wynter, it's fine…" I paused for thought "Not really, I mean, I remember bits and pieces, I was super young when my father adopted me…"

"Do you like being adopted?"

"Well, I don't really remember any different so I guess so…"

"I'm not adopted but Wynter, Cleo and I have different dads, Wynter doesn't know who hers is though…"

"Alright Alma, that's enough…" Wynter interjected, she seemed uncomfortable as her face burned red and she clasped her hands in front of her tightly. I wondered how Wynter dealt with the weight of the world crushing the weight of her body.

"Well… I better get these home to bed…" She piped up.

"Can't we stay for a bit longer?" Alma pulled on Wynters arm, her eyes longing.

"Alma, another day, Cleo is practically falling asleep"

They left without another word, I was alone again.

I heard my father come in early morning, his keys on the side table in the hall, his boots being kicked into the cupboard, the sound of his careless footsteps down the stairs, I pretended to be asleep as he crouched down next to me, he caressed my arm with the back of his hand causing me to shudder.

"Violet...." He whispered, close to my face, his husky voice echoing in my ear. "Wake up, I have something to tell you..."
I pretended to wake up, opening my eyes slowly, stretching slightly and then sitting up, my father dropped to his knees, taking both my hands in his.

"What is it?" I asked, my voice shaking but with a sense of intrigue.

"I was thinking of adopting you a sibling..."
My eyes lit up and I could feel a soft smile on route to my face, I would no longer be alone, maybe it would be a sister, like Wynter, we'd chat late into the night like best friends, draw together, tell each other everything, or maybe it would be a brother, we'd rough house, play ball games that kind of stuff, a sibling? I thought, would be perfect.

"Would you like that Violet?" My father held my hands tighter, smiling his crooked yellow smile.
I nodded and he pulled me into a hug, maybe things were looking up, maybe everything was going to be okay.

"Father..." I started "Thank you..."
I felt his grip tighten on me again, not in a comforting kind of way, in a possessive kind of way, but I didn't mind too much, soon I wouldn't be by myself, soon I would have a sibling.

WYNTER

As I placed Cleo down onto the mattress, she stirred but didn't wake up, Alma had spent the entire way home from Violet's telling me she wasn't tired through her yawns but as soon as she hit the bed she was out like a light, I pulled the blanket up to their chins planted a kiss on each of their foreheads and took my usual place by the window, the moon was full that night and so vibrant it practically lit up the entire room. The night was peaceful, after raining and storming all evening it was the first time in a long time I felt at peace, but that piece was shattered as soon as it came as I heard my mother crashing through the front door.

"Wynter!" She shrieked, her voice shrill and cold. I jumped up quickly entering the living room and closing Cleo and Alma in.

"Mama, the kids are asleep, you have to keep your voice down…"

The smell of alcohol hit me like a closed fist punch as soon as I entered the room, she was staggering over her feet, grabbing onto every piece of furniture as she walked, her makeup had began running off her face and her lipstick was smudged. Thank God that social worker didn't see this.

"What lies have you been spreading about me?"

"What? I haven't, honest"

"I saw your teacher tonight and she gave me a mouthful, at the bar, my place to relax and unwind and I can't even escape you brats for one second…"

At first I was bewildered and then slightly comforted that Miss Larkin cared enough about me to defend me.

"wipe that smile of your face or I'll do it for you…"

I didn't even realise I had been smiling.

"I didn't say anything to Miss Larkin, I promise."
"You didn't?"
"No, I don't want our family to be broken up... But don't you think you'd make it harder for them to take us kids away if you maybe laid off the alcohol, maybe got a job?" I bit my lip anxiously, my mother fell silent, for a moment she seemed human, she slumped down on the sofa, defeated and placed her head into her hands. I stood frozen to the spot before hesitantly taking a seat next to her.

"You can do it..." I whispered "I believe in you..."
"I'm not sure I can..." She lifted her head, her tear-stained cheeks flushed pink "I'm an awful mama..."
"No you're not, nobody's perfect mama, but please, we don't wanna have to bury you before we become adults"
"I'm scared Wynter..."
"Me too Mama..."
My mother laid her head on my lap like I was the mother and she child, I stroked her hair, we stayed like that for the rest of the night.

I woke up early on the Saturday morning of that week, the sun was scorching in the sky and for once it felt warm against my skin as it beamed in our bedroom window. Genevieve had invited me over to her house to hang out for the day, just me and her, like old times. I remembered being really young, 5 or 6, Genevieve and I used to spend all of our weekends, all day Saturday and Sunday together, playing at the park, climbing trees, having dinner at her house, as there wasn't much food at my own house, they were fond memories.

"Wynter..." Genevieve shook my shoulders to bring me back to earth. "You're day dreaming...."
"Sorry..."
"Is everything okay?" She asked, concern written on

her face "My mother told me about…"

"Yeah, things are getting better…" I rushed the conversation on. "So last I heard you had a boyfriend…" Genevieve blushed "C'mon G, tell me everything!"

"His name is Jacob Byers, he goes to my judo class, and…" She came close to my ear "He's 13…"

"Oooooh, an older man…"

Genevieve and I made our way into the little village strip in the middle of Sherwood where they had shops, clothes shops, toy shops, little independent businesses that kind of stuff. I didn't have any money, but I had mastered the art of window shopping. On every streetlight, a purple ribbon was tied, I hadn't seen that before, I wondered what it meant. I reached my hand out and pulled the ribbon, it came undone easily and felt soft as I weaved it through my fingers.

"What's all this about?" I turned to Genevieve, she shrugged and we walked on.

"C'mon Wynter, let's go in here," Genevieve grabbed me by the hand a dragged me into a small clothing store that was run by a family who lived just up the road from my house, much different from the second hand store my mother got all of my clothes from. There was a pair of blue fabric shorts with darker blue striped and a belt tied around them, $7.50, $4.40 more than I had.

"They're nice Wynter, are you going to get them, they'd suit you…"

"no, I uh, don't have the funds." I laughed, trying to attempt to hide my embarrassment, but I could tell she could see right through it as she offered me a sympathetic smile, the kind people gave me when they felt sorry for me.

"What do you think?" She held a bright pink pleated dress against herself and twirled around, the dress wasn't to my taste but it suited her.

"It's nice…"

She smiled and tucked the dress under her arm to continue looking, disappearing into the clothing abyss. I was still curious about the purple ribbon, was it a celebration I didn't know about? Genevieve reappeared moments later, her arms so full she could barely see past all the items she had, she dumped them down at the cashiers desk.

"Is that everything?" The lady asked, she was of Indian descent and in her mid-40s, short, not much taller than myself. Her eyes were dark and expressive they crinkled at the corners when she smiled. Her clothes were beautiful and vibrant, a bright purple dress with some pale blue accents, her jet-black hair was tied back into a tight and tidy bun, a few jasmine flowers sticking out from it with large hoop earrings that grazed her shoulders. She had a warm smile, a welcoming smile.

"Yes that's all…"

"Nothing for you deary?" She turned her attention to me, silently I shook my head and she began scanning Genevieve's items.

"That'll be $62 please…"

Genevieve handed the money over the counter took her items and we began to walk away, but something was playing on my mind and |I just couldn't shake it.

"Excuse me…" I turned back "Do you know what all the purple ribbons are for?"

The lady behind the counter handed me a newspaper, the front page made my heart sink to my toes, I felt sick.

"Wynter, are you okay? You look a little green…"

"Yeah, I'm fine, I just remembered, I have to pick my sisters up, I better go"

Without another word I darted for the door, newspaper in hand and down the street, running so fast I could feel my thighs burning, it couldn't be true, maybe I was wrong, I really hoped I was.

Sherwood Library was situated towards the entrance to the national park, it was an old building but had an aura of Victorian elegance around it, a symphony of red brick and limestone with large windows. I rarely came here, but I didn't have a computer at home and I was in dire need of one to use. I climbed the giant stairs up to the large wooden doors, they were heavy, and entered into the main foyer, it was bathed in natural light, the marble floor echoing my footsteps like it was haunted, there was a desk where the librarian sat, a woman in her late 60's early 70's, she seemed like she was part of the furniture, like she had heard some stories in her time. Her hair was grey and wiry and she dawned a pair of round golden glasses, she looked up from her paperwork upon my entrance and offered a warm smile.

"I'm just here to use the computer..." I handed her a $1 bill.

"Take your pick sweetie.." She spoke in in a hushed tone.

I nodded and head through the main reading area. Towers and towers of books, old and new on shelves that stretched all the way up to the ceiling, like skyscrapers in the big city. The air carried the scent of aged paper, ink and polished wood. I entered the computer room, there were 4 computers and all were available, I sat at the one on the far end. As I waited for it to power up, I held the newspaper I had gotten from the lady at the shop in my trembling hands. I knew I recognized the person on the front cover, but I truly hoped I was wrong. Okay, here goes, my fingers began typing before waiting for the searches to appear. That's when I saw it. "10 YEARS ON FROM THE DISAPPEARANCE OF 3-YEAR-OLD EMILY MYERS, LABELLED AS THE GIRL IN THE VIOLET

DRESS BY THE MEDIA, HER FAMILY SAY THEY WILL NEVER GIVE UP HOPE ON THEIR SEARCH FOR THEIR BUBBLY LITTLE GIRL…"

I sat back in my chair, my teeth sticking to my lips, my palms sweaty, my heart racing. "THE GIRL IN THE VIOLET DRESS." "VIOLET". The picture, it was the same picture Violet had up on the shelf in the living room. The basement, it wasn't just the basement, it was her prison. She wasn't dyslexic, she was never taught, she wasn't just clumsy, she was being hurt. My heart began to swell in my chest, pulsing like I had just ran a marathon. What was I going to do? Violet wasn't just living a complicated life like myself, she was a missing child. In an instant I hit print, grabbed the paper from the printer and raced for the door. I knew what I had to do.

VIOLET

Since my father told me about the potential for a little sibling, I couldn't stop thinking about it. I had some memory of a sister I had from my biological family, but no memories of anything we did together, it would be nice to have some company during the times Wynter couldn't be here, I thought.

"Father..." I called excitedly as he ascended the stairs "When you decide on my little sibling that you're going to adopt, can I come?"

"Not now Violet."

He seemed frustrated and harassed.

"What's wrong?"

"I've been let go from my job, that's what..." He spat the words as he said them, before sitting down next to me.

"I'm sorry..."

There was no talking him down when he was like this, I reached out to tap his shoulder, but decided against it at the last moment, as I brought my arm back to my side, I heard a tear, the seam of my dress had come undone under the arm, my father heard it too because he jumped to his feet.

"Great! Do you know how lucky you are you little brat, I feed you..." *Barley.* "I clothe you" *Yeah, one dress every two years or so* "and what thanks do I get?" My father scoffed, yanking me to my feet by my wrist with a grip as tough as barbed wire, he shook me by the shoulders to the point I really thought my head would fall clean off.

"Please, I don't need a dress, it's fine!" I begged him as he shoved me full force into the brick wall, dizzying me. I lay there, in the foetal position, every blow feeling like my brain would slip out through my ear, I imagined myself some place different, I was in a field, the spring daffodils in full bloom, I'm running, running, a woman opens her arms to me, she feels like a mother, sweet, comforting, she pulls me into a warm embrace. "It's okay." She tells me, her voice gentle, smooth like butter. Then I opened my eyes, it had gotten dark, my head felt funny and I couldn't remember why I was lying on the ground. I struggled to my feet, the pain intense, I suddenly caught a glimpse of my reflection in the tiny basement window, I didn't even recognise the broken and bruised girl standing in front of me.

I heard the basement door open; it startled me awake but I pretended to be asleep, he'd go away if I was sleeping.

"Violet…" A voice whispered, a voice that wasn't my father but I recognised it, even in the dark.
I sat up in my bed and watched as Wynter emerged from the shadows, I could only make out half of her face, but that half of her face seemed concerned, like something was worrying her.

"Violet, I need to tell you something…"
I still wasn't sure if I was dreaming or if I was awake, I rubbed my eyes but she didn't disappear.

"What is it Wynter?"
Wynter reached into her bag and pulled out a torch, she shone it on me.

"What happened to your face?"

"It's a long story, what did you need to tell me?"
Wynter lowered the torch, she handed me a couple of sheets of paper and bowed her head. I hadn't been reading for very long but I could make out a few words.
"MISSING" "VIOLET" "GIRL" "MOTHER" "SISTER" "FIND HER". Next to the words was a picture, it was a picture of me, the one from when I was little.

"What does it say…"

"You might want to sit down?"
We both sat down on the floor, I was so anxious I didn't even notice how cold it was on my skin.

"Wynter, you're scaring me... Wait, how did you get past my father?"

"That's not important right now... He's not your father..."

"Well of course not, I'm adopted, but he's pretty much my father"

"That's what I mean, Violet, listen to me, you weren't adopted..."

"What do you mean?"

Wynter took a deep breath, her eyes wide but blank, my heart stopped and swelled inside my chest, tightening with angst.

"You were taken..." The words jumped out her mouth and slapped me in the face.

"Wynter I don't understand..."

"Your biological parents, they've been looking for you, for 10 years Violet, they've never given up... I can help you go home!"

"No, it's not true!" I tore the paper in half and threw it to the wind. "I think I would remember if I was taken..."

"Maybe not..."

"You should go..."

"Violet, please..."

"No, you're a liar and I hate you!"

The anger bubbled up in me like lava in a volcano, I wasn't really sure why, but in that moment, it didn't matter, I just wanted to be alone. I didn't hate Wynter, I loved her, but I was angry, I was furious, I was scared.

"Violet..." Wynters voice began to break, tears streaming down and staining her cheeks.

"Go!"

She stood for a moment before about turning and slowly walking away, up the stairs and disappearing into the darkness. I fell to my knees, suddenly feeling heavy, grabbing the torn paper I pieced it together, he was my father he had to be. I shoved the paper under the bed and laid down. The darkness seemed to swallow me whole, like a monster that might hide under the bed or in the closet, all of sudden I felt alone.

PEYTON

I wasn't in the building for 5 minutes before I got called to the see principal, like a naughty schoolgirl. I was greeted in the office by a very unenthused Mrs Holden, sitting in her big leather chair.

"Take a seat Peyton…."

I knew what it was about, I didn't know how I was going to explain my way out of this one.

"If this is about Friday night…"

"I'll do the talking…" She interrupted, sternly.

Mrs Holden had been my teacher back when I went to this school, before she became principal, she was just as scary now as she was then.

"Sorry…" I retreated into my shell.

"What do you think you were playing at? Approaching a child's parent outside of school? Especially a child as complex as Wynter… How do you think that makes our establishment look?"

"I'm sorry. I really thought I was doing what was best for Wynter, her mother was supposed to be getting clean, she was drinking and no doubt had left those kids alone at home"

"That is not your job Peyton, your job is to teach, that is all… I have no choice but to suspend you for a few days…"

"What?!?!"

"Lara will take your class until you come back…. Now, please go, I have to put out some fires that you started…"

I rose from my seat slowly, I wasn't sure if I was hoping she'd change her mind or if I was trying to pretend it wasn't happening but I left without looking back and closed the door behind me.

As I was leaving the school, I saw her, my every instinct told me not to approach her, but my heart ignored me and I made my way over to Wynter Jones as she sat by herself on the bench in the middle of the playground. Her eyes were heavy and she seemed like she had a lot on her mind. I perched down beside her.

"Something on your mind Wynter?"

She kept her head bowed and kicked her legs that couldn't reach the ground back and forth under the bench.

"Just stuff…" She said, finally, but still she didn't take her eyes off the ground, like she was watching something and was worried if she took her eyes of it, it would disappear.

"Same her Wynter, same here…"

She looked up at me, her eyes red raw as if she'd been crying, she looked perplexed as she looked me up and down.

"Are you going somewhere Miss Larkin?"

"Yeah, I'm, uh, taking some time off…"

"Why?"

I bit my lip, the first rule of being a teacher is keeping your personal life personal.

"Just some personal reasons" I told her, standing up. "Well I'd best be getting off"

I began to turn and walk away; I felt her arms around my waist.

"Thank you" She said

"What for"

"I know what you did, and since you spoke to her, Mama hasn't even had one drop of alcohol…"

I smiled to myself because I felt like I had achieved something, I held her tiny frame tight in my arms, she seemed frail, delicate, but also lighter than she had ever been before.

WYNTER

    I thought about Violet a lot over the next few days, her black and blue eyes, the dried blood in her nostrils, her face when she was telling me to leave, it broke me inside, how could I get her to believe me? What would it take? Should I go to the police? No, Violet would never forgive me, I had to fix this on my own. I sat in my room pondering my thoughts as I gave Cleo her bottle, suddenly, the bedroom door burst open and my mother appeared, grinning from ear to ear. She had been a lot better recently, more coherent, more like a normal mother, her baby bump had grown a lot and looked more like an actual baby than a food baby now.

    "Wynter, guess what!" She began dancing around the room to a song only she could here. "I got a job!" With the shock, I dropped Cleos bottle onto the floor and froze in the spot, in a dream state, I couldn't talk, I couldn't move, were things really getting better? Was my childhood entering into its "normal" phase? My mother had gotten a job, something she had never been able to hold down, she hadn't drank a dop of alcohol in days and she had started walking Alma to school in the mornings so I didn't have to. I felt a smile edge onto my face as she stood in front of me awaiting my reaction.

    "For real?" I whispered.

    "For real…"

I jumped to my feet with excitement, placed Cleo down onto the mattress and threw my arms around my mother, she tightened her arms around my waist and for the first time in a long time, I felt comforted, I felt at peace, but it all drained from my bones as I remembered Violet, I loosened my grip and sat back down.

    "What's wrong Wynter, I thought you'd be happy…" My mother sat down next to me, picking Cleo up onto her lap and rocking her to sleep.

"No, I am, I am happy, it's just…"

"What?"

I couldn't tell her the full truth, she'd never have believed me.

"Well, I have this friend, she's sort of, in trouble?"

"What kind of trouble?"

"Enormous trouble, but she doesn't think she is, I need to convince her that she is so I can help her."

"Oh Wynter, you can't make people want help, she has to realise it herself…"

"But what if she doesn't?"

"Then, you just have to be there for her… Like you've always been there for me"

Mama was right, I just had to be her friend, maybe then she may figure it out on her own, with my support of course, but first, I had to get her to forgive me. .

"Hey, do you mind taking Alma to school tomorrow, I really don't want to be late for my first day…I'll take Cleo to the child minder before I go…"

"Sure…"

"Hey, chin up kiddo, I'm sure your friend will be just fine…"

The next morning, I got myself and Alma changed for school, waved my mother off to her first day of her new job and headed for the road. Alma insisted on bringing her scooter that her father had bought her on their last outing so I knew it would take us twice as long to get there, but I didn't mind.

"Now that mama has a new job, will we move to a bigger house, with our own rooms, I'd paint mines pink…"

"Whoa, slow down tiger, no one is moving, we have to see if it works out first…"

"What do you mean?"

"Well Alma, mama doesn't have the best track

record..."

"I like our new mama better than our old mama..." Hearing Alma say that made my heart break into a million little pieces realising in her entire life, she had never seen our mother sober, that fact stung.

"She's still the same mama, just, less sick... She's getting better..."

"Oh..."

We rounded the corner onto the street where Alma's school stood, there was a car parked just up the road, a black one, the engine was running but it was stationary, it made me feel uneasy, Alma noticed it too because she stepped off of her scooter and clutched my hand, as we got closer and closer, I recognised him, the driver, it was Violet's father, I mean, the guy who took her. He was watching us, our every move, with his dark sinister eyes, did he know about me? How I had been sneaking into his house when he wasn't there? How I had been the one sneaking Violet out?

"Why is that man staring at us?" Alma queried, her eyes following him like he was following us.

"I have no idea..."

He rolled down his window and made eye contact with me, just as he did, he placed his sun glasses on and sped off. The exchange chilled me to the bone as I walked Alma to the school gate, I crouched down in front of her and took both her hands in mine.

"Alma, listen to me, after school, I want you to wait inside the gate, where a grown up can see you and wait for me or mama to pick you up, okay?"

"Okay..."

"Alma, I mean it, you have to do as I say..."

"Wynter, I got it..."

I kissed her on the head and gave her one last squeeze before watching her walk through the gates.

School was weird without Miss Larkin, empty almost, Miss Giles was a great and all but Miss Larkin understood me in a way that no one else had, it was because of her I got my mother back. I sat down at my desk, I could feel the eyes burning into the back of my head, news travelled fast in this town, so I knew everyone knew of my situation, the hushed whispers behind my back, the sympathetic looks, it made me want to disappear into the ground.

"Hey" Genevieve appeared at the desk next to me, she didn't usually sit there but she was today "Where did you run off to the other day?"

"I just had some personal business…"

"What kind of personal business…"

"The personal kind" I snapped "Sorry, I'm just, having a bad day…"

"It happens, Wynter, I'm going to ask you one question, and I want you to be honest okay?" I hated it when questions started like that, like I was about to be put on the spot. "is everything all good at home, your mother and everything?"

"Yeah everything is good." For the first time ever, it wasn't a lie.

"Alright, everyone turn to page 316…"

As soon as the bell rang for the end of school I was out of there like a puff of smoke. I ran full speed to Alma's school to meet her, panting, I entered through the gates, where we'd agreed to meet, but she wasn't there, I entered into the school but her teacher said she had left, that's when the panic set in, what if she had been taken? My heart was palpitating and my palms were dripping in sweat, that's when I saw her, by the car that was watching us earlier in the day, talking to the man who had taken Violet. My body felt a burning sense of dread tingling all over, and I ran towards my sister life my life depended on it, hers definitely did.

"Alma, no!" I shrieked as I filtered through the crowds of kids leaving through the school gates with their parents, when I reached her I grabbed her by the hand harshly and pulled her to my side.

"Wynter, this is Marcus, he's really nice…"
I studied his face, every line and wrinkle, every mole and imperfection and stored them inside my brain. What did he want from us?

"I can give you a lift home if you'd like…"

"No" I said as I pulled Alma further from the car "We'd rather walk…"
After staring Marcus down one last time I left with Alma, not letting go of her hand the whole down the street, as we approached Violet's house (or should I say prison) I was stopped in my tracks.

"Wynter!" Violet approached the gates, clutching an iron bar in each hand. I couldn't believe that she was outside in the world and not simply confined to her little basement room. "I'm sorry I yelled at you before, can we be friends again?"
I smiled to myself and reached through the bars to take her hand.

"Friends… What are you doing out here, I thought you weren't allowed…"

"My father has me doing yard work, pulling weeds and stuff, it's sort of my punishment, but he is trusting me more because I haven't snuck out in a while…"
Violet still looked worse for wear, one of her eyes was swollen shut but had turned slightly yellow, which I think meant it was healing, her ankles were red raw and the skin had started to peel off from the ropes chafing her skin and somehow she had gotten even thinner.

"Punishment for what?"

"I tore my dress… My father lost his job so he

can't pay for another one, plus I wet the bed last night. I was careless, I deserve to be punished."
Violet pulled at her earlobes when she was nervous and avoided eye contact I squeezed her hand gently, the bones in her hand jagging into my own.

"I'm glad we're friends again..."

I didn't tell her about Marcus showing up to Alma's school to watch us, or how he was chatting with Alma and offering us a lift home, she was hurting and I didn't want to make it any worse.

VIOLET

As punishment, sometimes my father wouldn't feed me for days, one time it was a week, sometimes the hunger was so great it was agony whenever my stomach rumbled. One time it got so bad I snuck food, that's why he put locks on the cupboards and fridge and boy did I get it that night. I felt weak as I rose to my feet, I picked up a stone that I had sharpened and began etching into the wall, it was like having a piece of chalk and it meant I could make my room more homely. I wrote my name in big capital letters across the wall, VIOLET, but every time I reached my arm up the tear in my dress got bigger and bigger. My foot grazed something underneath my bed, I crouched down and pulled out the pieces of the torn newspaper article, Wynter had brought me, I studied it, that was my picture, but there must have been some mistake.

"Violet..." My father called from the top of the stairs, I stopped what I was doing, paralysed with fear, I gulped hard shoved the paper back under my bed and moved slowly towards the stairs. "Violet!!!"
I sped up, startled by the grit in his voice, when I saw his face, he seemed surprisingly happy, I was sceptical, because I had been burned before.

"What is it father?"

"I have the best news," He paused for thought before placing a hand on both of my shoulders "I found you a sibling"

"You did, is it a boy or a girl..."

"It's a surprise, come on..."

"Where?"

"you're going to meet your new sibling..."
Happiness filled my bones like air in a balloon, I felt like I was floating, I was finally not going to be alone.

I had never been allowed to go on the other side of the fence, this was the first time I actually had permission. My father put one of his coats on me and put up the hood, he lifted me from the house to his car and bundled me in.
    "Put your seatbelt on..."
I had no idea what that meant, my father rolled his eyes and clipped something over my lap, he said it was to keep me safe. I jumped when the car revved to a start, like an angry lion and then we started moving. We travelled for several minutes, up the street, back down the street, round the corner, and then we parked up. I had no idea where we were but I had never seen so many other children in my life, what were they all doing here and where were they going? Was this some sort of adoption place? Was this where my father got me? We sat in silence, waiting and waiting. Kids came and kids went, I wondered which kid would be my brother or sister.
    "There, there she is!"
She? I was getting a sister? I followed my father's finger to see who he was pointing to before my heart sank.
    "Are you sure that's her?"
    "Positive, she's perfect..."
I could physically feel my heart breaking inside my chest, it was then I knew she was right, Wynter, she was right about everything.

    On the way home, my father explained to me his plan to acquire my new sister, he had to make some arrangements before picking her up and taking her home, he had to make her up a bed, he had just gotten a new job, so he had to wait for his first pay check so he could support us all. He was buzzing, climbing the walls, I had never seen him so excited.
    "What if she doesn't want to come home with us?" I asked.

"She will..."
I watched as the outside world that I rarely got to see whizzed by in a blur of colours, I wondered when the next time I got to see it would be, if I'd ever get to see it again.

"What if I don't want a new sibling?"
"I thought you were so excited..."
"I was, I am..."
"it'll all be good in time."
The clogs in my brain were working overtime, planning, plotting, scheming, I needed Wynter, I needed her brain.

After the fall of darkness, after my father had fallen asleep, I snuck out to the yard, the cold air chilled me to the bone and I could barely feel my feet. I waited, wondering if Wynter would come, like she used to. I waited and waited and just when I thought she wouldn't appear, I recognised her outline in the moonlight and breathed a sigh of relief. She appeared out of the darkness her face serious.

"Violet I have something I need to tell you..." She paused, "Your father, he's been showing up to my sisters school, watching me and Alma... He was there yesterday and he was there again today..."

"he's not my father... Wait, that was a school?"
"Violet..."
"I was there today Wynter, I was promised a sibling, y'know, to keep me company and stuff, I was so excited, he took me out this morning, he wants to take Alma... I'm so sorry Wynter... I, I, I didn't know... You were right, about everything..."

"We have to get you out of there, before it's too late"

"how? He's fixed the gaps in the fence and it's way too high to get over... And when I got out, I don't even know where I would go, Wynter I'm really scared..."

"I promise I won't let anything happen to you..."

"I've read a little bit about your family on the internet, do you want to know about them?"

I nodded. Wynter told me how my mother was called April and my father was called Lewis and how I had an older sister called Eleanor who was now 17 and I was called Emily and since I was taken my mother had another child called Erica who was just 3 years old, the age I was when I was stolen. She told me how my father worked as a heart doctor and my mother owned a bakery called "Sweet treats". She told me how they'd never stopped searching for me, in the 10 years I was gone, they never gave up. That I was in fact 13 years old, 2 years older than Wynter. How the police had stopped looking for a person and had started looking for a body. I bowed my head, the tears fizzing in my eyes, stinging.

"I'm so sorry Violet..."

"What am I gonna do?" I rubbed the tears as they cascaded from my eyes down my cheeks.

"we need a plan..."

"A plan?"

"we're gonna get you out of there?"

"How? He's really tightened everything up around here, there's no way out. Besides, What if my family don't like me?"

"There's no way."

Wynter reached her arm through the bars and took mine, her hand was ice cold and she was trembling but in some ways it was comforting, in other ways, terrifying.

"Wynter, I need to go back inside, before he notices I'm gone..."

"Wait, meet me here, not tomorrow, but the next day, 8 o'clock at night, okay?"

"I can't tell the time..."

"Here..." Wynter rolled up her sleeve, taking off a

thing that she called a watch, she handed it through the bars to me, it was light blue and had numbers on it and three moving lines, one that kept going round and round and another two that only moved occasionally.

"I can't tell time..."

"It's my watch, not tomorrow, the next day, when the small hand hits the 8 and the big hand hits the 12, and when it gets dark outside, that's when I will meet you here, okay?"

"Okay... Wait, what's the plan?"

"Leave it with me..."

"Wynter..."

"Do you trust me?"

I nodded and watched as Wynter bounded away, with a new-found purpose I had never seen before. I did trust Wynter, but I was afraid, not long ago, I didn't even know I had a family who were looking for me, but now I did but what if I never got to see them? What if I was stuck here forever, or worse?

WYNTER

My head was filled with the promise I had made Violet, I was going to get her out of there but how? I was an 11-year-old girl who's own life was messy, that didn't qualify me to help, but I wanted to desperately, if not for Violet, for Alma. Since I had learned of his plans, I had never let her out of my sight. I walked her to school; I walked her home from school and she wasn't allowed out to play alone.

"Wynter you're tugging!" Alma squirmed as I ran the brush through her tuggy hair.

"If you keep moving it'll make it worse Alma... Sit still... Even Cleo sits still to get her hair done..."

"That's because she has like 3 strands..."
I chuckled to myself, Alma was growing up so fast, becoming more independent, not needing me as much, it was the same for my mother, since she started her new job and stopped drinking as much, she had stepped into the mother role, a role I had played practically my whole life, I was happy for her, but sometimes, I did miss being needed. I ran my fingers through Alma's hair, remembering when she was just a baby, she had hardly any hair, it was white blonde, she cried more than Cleo, so I'd sit with her through the night, wrapped up in a blanket, rocking her until she eventually drifted off. My mother would be out for days at a time during that time so Alma never really did connect with her.

"Alright, your turn missy..." I lifted Cleo over and sat her in between my legs, at that moment my mother walked in.

"I can get Cleo ready Wynter..."
My mother lifted Cleo causing her to erupt into deafening screams, squirming, hitting, trying to break free. My mother tried to sooth her but Cleo wasn't having it, she reached

for me, grabbing the air with her little hands.

"What's wrong with her?" My mother had a panicked expression on her face as she attempted to get Cleo under control, eventually after moments of fighting it, she handed her back to me and Cleo buried her head into my neck and muttered "Mama..."
My mother looked defeated, like she had just been punched in the stomach and all of the air had escaped from her, she sat down on the floor next to me.

"My baby girl hates me..."
"She doesn't hate you..."
"She does..."
"She just doesn't know you..."
"What if this new baby doesn't like me?"
"This baby, will get the mama you are now, something Alma, Cleo and I didn't get, the new baby will love you, just as much as we do, okay? I promise."
I pulled Cleos vest over her head causing what little hair she had to stand up on the top of her head. My mother put her head in her hands and began to cry, I placed Cleo down onto the mattress and placed an arm around my mother, I could feel her shaking beneath me.

"We love you mama..." Alma chimed in as she climbed onto mama's knee. It was the first time I had felt a part of a real family.

1 day and 9 hours until operation "save Violet" and I still didn't have a plan and as the bell rang for the start of class my thoughts couldn't focus, they were racing, relentlessly galloping in circles around my brain. The room fell into a blur, a kaleidoscope of colours and faces all blending into one, my heart palpitating and my body feeling the weight of the promise I had made Violet, crushing me beneath its mass. I clutched onto the side of the desk with both hands to distract myself.

"Good morning class..." Miss Giles spoke over the

hushed chatter of my classmates; the class fell silent and I could finally think. "Now, today is my last day as your teacher, Miss Larkin returns tomorrow… So today, I thought we'd put a few things together for her return." Miss Giles wanted us to make cards for Miss Larkin coming back and a banner, I didn't know why Miss Larkin was absent, but I did worry that is was something to do with me.

"What are you doing?" Genevieve scooted over next to me.

"No idea, I'm no good at art…"

"Wynter, you're a borderline genius but you can't figure out what to do?"

It was in that moment, it came to me, the plan, it was risky but it just could work, if I could pull it off.

At recess I spent my time mind mapping, listing and scheming, in a secluded area of the playground, jotting ideas down in my journal.

"Looks important…" She was everywhere, Genevieve appeared as if from out of nowhere, like she was spying on me. I slammed shut my journal.

"It isn't…" I insisted.

"Wynter, I'm worried about you…"

"I'm fine…"

Genevieve, annoyingly, no matter what stage we were in our friendship, always knew when something was on my mind, and these days there was always something on my mind. I sighed, succumbing to the fact I was going to have to tell her the truth because I knew Genevieve and she wasn't going to give up.

"I found out what the purple ribbons were for…" I started

"Yeah, didn't the lady in the shop say they were for some missing kid?"

"Yeah, but I looked into it more, it's not just any

missing kid, it's Violet..."

"Your friend? Wynter I don't understand..."

"Violet is the missing kid..."

Genevieve's expression dropped and her face turned chalk white.

"We have to tell someone Wynter..."

"No..." I grabbed her wrist as she tried to leave and pulled her back to my side. "You can't, I have a plan, I'm going to get her out..."

"That look on your face tells me your plan isn't just go to the police?"

"The man who has her, he's really dangerous..."

"Remind me why you can't just tell someone, like an adult, or…. the police?"

"Who's gonna believe an 11 year old?"

"You do have a point..."

"Besides, I have to be the one to save her, I owe her that much, and I promised G, I promised her.."

"Please be careful..."

"Promise you won't tell anyone, swear it, at least until tomorrow night..."

"fine..."

"Spit swear?"

I spat into the palm of my hand and offered it to her, she hesitated before doing the same and we shook on it.

My mother was picking Alma and Cleo up so I walked home alone, a worry in the pit of my stomach the whole way there hoping that Alma would be there, that my mother had remembered to meet her inside the gate, that Alma hadn't gone off with any strangers. As I approached the house I breathed a sigh of relief when I saw my mother, Cleo and Alma laughing and playing through the window, I felt a smile fade onto my face as I stopped in my tracks to watch, it had been something I was dreaming of, my mother to be on her sober journey, my sisters to be happy and for me to stand down my mothering duties and get to be a kid, My mother spotted me through the window and waved me in.

"We're playing dodge ball, but with cushions…" Alma giggled with delight as she ducked behind the couch, my mother was hiding behind the kitchen counter, cushion in hand, she hurtled it across the room, it hit the wall and Alma bounced up.

"Missed me!" She yelled but my mother grabbed another cushion and threw it, hitting alma on the thigh.

"Gotcha!"

It felt too good to be true, like I might wake up suddenly and things would be back to the way they were, but I would enjoy it whilst it lasted.

"Can I put the girls to bed tonight Wynter?" My mother asked, I smiled and nodded as she threw her arms around me, in a warm embrace, I melted into her arms feeling suddenly safe and content.

I sat in the corner of the room doing my homework, the faint sound of light and laughter echoing from the other side of the room. I never got to do this, just sit back and do my homework, I was always doing it last minute. I looked up from my math homework to see my mother sitting by Alma and Cleo's bedside, telling them a story, they were hanging on her every word.

"the princess was the most beautiful in all the land" My mother told.

"What was her name Mama?" Alma asked, an inquisitive look on her face. My mother stroked her chin and looked around, her eyes eventually falling on me, she offered me a comforting smile.

"Her name is Wynter, and she's a very special princess, she's selfless, always taking care of others, even when they don't deserve it."

I let my math book fall and I leaned in to hear the rest

of the story, I was invested, I needed to know how it would end, did Wynter finally get the life that she always dreamt of? It was certainly starting to seem that way. My mother tucked Alma and Cleo in, their eyes were beginning to go droopy, the way they always did when they were tired and she grabbed my hand gently, motioning me to follow her through to the other room, I did as I was told.

"Guess what," she said in a hushed tone.
"What?"
"I wanted you to be the first to know, but I found out the gender of the baby!"
My mother pursed her lips and stood back, awaiting my reaction, most of the time I was trying to forget about it, I didn't want another baby sibling, not now, not when things were going so well. Her face dropped when she didn't get the reaction she was expecting.

"Wynter, I thought you'd be happy…"
"I am it's just… it's not my baby, it's yours"
"She's our baby Wynter…"
"She? You're having another girl?"

PEYTON

After my "leave of absence" I couldn't have been happier to get back to work, I had spent my days watching reality TV, planning activities for my class and wallowing in self-pity.

"Pey!" Lara swung me around by the arms almost pulling me off my feet. "how are you?"

"Yeah, I'm fine, thanks…"

"As lovely as your class are, I am really glad you're back…"

I walked tentatively down the hall, wondering who all knew about my discipline, was it the talk of the school or were people blissfully unaware? My class looked exactly the same as when I left it, it was like the last few days hadn't happened, I sat down in my chair and took it all in. My thoughts were interrupted by the bell and the chaotic filter of children rushing through the door.

"Morning Miss…" They echoed as they all took their seats at their desk, then Lara appeared at the door and offered a signal to little Ross Wilmington as he used a string to roll down a large piece of paper that read "WELCOME HOME MISS LARKIN" with a whole host of doodles on it, signed by every single child. I felt myself welling up.

"They made you cards too…" Lara nodded towards a wicker box filled to the brim with beautiful decorate cards.

"Thank you…" I wiped the tears from my eyes, my favourite part about teaching was the bond you were able to make each child and it was moments like this that I knew that I had made an impact.

"Wynter do you have a moment?" I called her as the rest of the children rushed out of the classroom for recess, like a bunch of caged animals at feeding time. She nodded and tentatively approached my desk.

"I just wanted to see how things were going, at home?"

Wynter shuffled her feet uncomfortably, she was an paradox, Wynter Jones, she was a vibrant spirit encased in a fragile cocoon. Her intelligence, like a hidden gem, sparkled against the backdrop of adversity, Wynter's mind was a constellation of brilliance, curiosity fuelled her, in class she was always first finished her work, and her work was never wrong, her mind had the precision of a watchmaker, yet her confidence was low, she was shy and modest, more of an observer like she wanted to think things through thoroughly before acting, this was perhaps due to her hardships, her mother was a captive of the bottle, weaving a web of chaos that had entrapped Wynter within it but she seemed resilient, like she always bounced back no matter what. Sometimes, her name felt ironic, Wynter, she longed for warmth, the kind that didn't burn and dreamt of snowflakes that didn't melt, but she was her own frost, it protected her from harm, no one could hurt her if she was icy cold and hard.

"Everything is good..." She offered a smile.

"are you sure?"

She nodded, seeming sincere.

"I just wanted to apologise to you, Wynter, about what happened between me and your mother, it was unprofessional and I'm sorry..."

"Haven't you read my card?"

"No, not yet..."

"read it..."

Wynter picked out a card from the box, on the front was quite a poorly sketched picture of two people (Wynter was clearly an academic, not a creative...), I presumed one was me and the other was her, the card was covered in purple glitter that came off in my hands. I opened it.

Miss Larkin,
I know it's partly my fault that you've been suspended, Miss Giles said you're just sick, but I'm not dumb, but what you did, I really appreciate it, my mother has been doing better, she got a job, it doesn't pay that well but it's a start, she barely drinks anymore, she plays with Cleo and Alma and walks Alma to school when she can, sometimes I worry that I'm not needed anymore, but I know this is how it is supposed to be, so thank you.
Love Wynter xox

I knew this was hard for her, that she wasn't used to sharing her feelings so writing them down was the easiest way for her to do that. I felt a warm sensation in the pit of my stomach, that I was able to help even just one child. I pulled her into a warm embrace, she stayed in my arms for several moments, like she needed it for a long time so I didn't let go either, not until she did.

"You know Wynter, it was still my duty to report what happened?"

"I know, but mama is better now, she's doing really well, we're a family now, a real family..."

"Alright Wynter, go enjoy what's left of recess..." She smiled nodded and ran out to join her peers, I placed the card into the top drawer of my desk so that I could look at it whenever I felt that I wasn't doing a good job, to remind myself that I was.

My favourite subject to teach was English, in particular, writing, I loved seeing what my students would think up from their imagination, every once in a while I'd come across something really special.

"Alright class, today's assignment, is a fun one, I want little essay on what you are going to be up to this weekend, doesn't matter how boring you think it is..."
I weaved in and out the desks placing their writing jotters down on each of their desks.

"I don't just want a measly paragraph though; it has to be at least 2 pages..." I made my way back to the front of the class, "you can draw pictures as well if you want, just make it creative..."
Before I had even finished speaking they had started writing, I wondered what adventures they would be getting up to, maybe a bike ride with family, maybe visiting grandparents, maybe an extracurricular activity. I sat down at my desk watching as they scrawled, lines and lines of their truth, my eyes focused on Wynter, how did she spend her weekends? Was she telling the truth about her mother? Or was she just feeding me what I wanted to hear?

WYNTER

I knew what I needed to do and the whole way home from school I played my plan over and over in my head, praying it would work, worrying if it didn't, the clogs of my brain working overtime. The walk home seemed to take an age, my mother was collecting Alma and Cleo so I had nothing to break up my journey. I rounded the corner onto my street to find two cars I had never seen before parked outside my house.

"Wynter..." A voice called from across the road, as my eyes focused, I realised it was Dominic, and suddenly my body filled with rage. He crossed the road over to me.

"What do you want?"

"I just need to talk to you..."

"Come to try and ruin my life more, well I'll have you know, mama is sober, she's doing well, no thanks to you..."

"Wynter, please, you have to listen to me..."

"Why should I? You had no faith in her, you thought she was a screw up, and she's not, you thought she could never get better and she has.."

"Why are they here then?"

I turned my attention to the chaos that was happening inside my house and my heart sank to my feet. No, this wasn't happening. I pushed past Dominic and sped up the path to my house and burst through the front door. Alma was screaming bloody murder as she was being dragged from her room by a man and a woman, a woman I recognised as Stephanie, the social worker. Alma was putting up a fight, kicking and punching. Cleo was silent, clinging to a third person, another woman, she seemed dazed, sleepy. I looked around for my mother, but she was nowhere to be seen.

"You must be Wynter..." The woman holding Cleo

announced, she was young, no older than 30, her hair, bleach blond and stuffed messily into a ponytail, her eyes were big and dark, like a bug, she was wearing a badge, her name was "Casey Andrews". I pushed away her hand as she offered it to me to shake.

"My name is Casey, I'm a social worker..."
"I can read..."
"Of course you can..."
"Where is mama?"
"We got a call from one of your neighbours to say they could hear a child screaming for the majority of the day... Your sisters were left alone all day and I am lead to believe this is not the first time..."
"No, it's not true, mama is sober, she's been getting better, she has a job..."
"We found her at a bar Wynter, we've found a really nice couple who've agreed to take you in, on a temporary basis..."
"What? Foster care? No way!" I pushed past her "Get your hands off her!!!"
Stephanie and the man let Alma go and she ran into my arms, I lifted her up and rocked her back and forth as she whimpered, trembling beneath my arms, she gripped her arms around my neck resting her chin on my shoulder.

"Wynter, please, think of your sisters, this is what's best for them, and you..." Stephanie approached slowly, like I was some sort of wild animal, I backed away from her, holding Alma tight.

"She's fine, my mama is fine! She's better, she is, you're lying!" I shrieked, I wasn't sure if I was trying to get them to believe me or I was trying to convince myself. She'd let me down many times before, why would this time be any different? Because she promised, that's why... She had promised me lots over the years, most of which fell through, but this time she had proved she could do it, this time she said she'd do it, for me. The man, his name was Adam Carlson, or so his pass said, pulled Alma from my grasp and headed for the door with Casey, who was still clutching Cleo.

"Wynter!" Alma screamed, her voice breaking, I ran to the door and watched as they bundled my sisters into the car. I ran to the car door and as I tried to get in, Adam stopped me.

"Not you Wynter…"

"But, I thought we were going to stay with a couple…"

"You're going to stay with a couple, your sisters are being placed elsewhere…"

Stunned I gazed on as the car door was shut with my sisters inside, Alma, with tear-stained cheeks pressed her face and the palms of her hands up against the window, like she was trying to break through. I rested my palms on top of the glass against hers.

"It's going to be okay Alma, I'll make sure of it, okay? I won't let you down…"

"Wynter…" Stephanie pulled me back from the car "It's time to go…"

My heart broke into a million tiny pieces as I watched the car drive away, who was going to read my sisters to sleep every night? Who was going to play with Alma's hair when she was sad? Or sing Cleo's favourite song to soothe her?

"You did this, didn't you?" I turned to Dominic, who was watching from the sidelines and lunged for him, grabbing onto his shirt, Stephanie pulled me back.

"Wynter, please…"

"No! I hate you!"

I did hate him, I hated his interfering, I hated that he broke my mother's heart and I hated that he'd ruined everything, just as it was going so well. Stephanie put her arm around me and lead me to her car, I could feel the anger fizzing in me, but the fire was put out by an overwhelming sense of sadness. Stephanie shut the car door behind me and I watched as my home got smaller and smaller before fading into the distance.

VIOLET

The little hand was pointing to the 6 and the big hand was pointing to the three when my father came home, it was almost time. I slipped the watch that Wynter had given my underneath my mattress when I heard him descend the stairs.

"I have a present for you..." He held a brown paper bag in his hand and thrusted it into my hands. I was apprehensive, I didn't normally get presents so I felt it between my fingertips for several moments, it was soft. I reached my hand into the bag and touched the gentle material that was inside. I wondered if he was onto me, if this was a trap. He stood over me, grinning from ear to ear,.

"Well, hurry up and open it." He said, half irritated, half jovial.

I tore the bag as I removed the item from it, a folded pink mess of material draped over my hand, my father snatched it from me and held it up. A dress, pink in colour with long mesh sleeves and a white collar, it was beautiful, but what was the catch?

"Well, what do you think? Do you like it...?"

I smiled and nodded, I really did like it though I really didn't want to.

"It's beautiful"

"Go on then, try it on..."

Sheepishly I took the dress from him, slipped my old tattered dress off and put the new one on, it was a little big but it wasn't filthy and it wasn't ripped, so I was grateful. It was confusing, because I wanted to hate him for what he did, for robbing me of my childhood, but I couldn't, I just couldn't.

When the big hand hit the 6 and the little hand hit the 7, my father took his usual place on the couch by the TV, I knew he would be there for the next several hours. I sat on the cold floor of the basement getting lost in my thoughts, thoughts about my family, if they'd recognise me, if they'd even like me. What did they do for fun? Were they strict? I lay down staring up at the cracked and derelict ceiling, did they live in a house or an apartment?

"Soon, all your dreams will come true…" I whispered into the wind, hoping it would somehow find its way to my mother, father and sisters. The chill seeped through my thin clothes, numbing my bones, time was moving painfully slow like a snail on the concrete, each second elongated, mocking my desperation. I had spent endless days here, counting the cracks, the spider webs, anything to distract from the gnawing hunger and painful beatings. My breaths echoed, hollow and raspy, like the room itself was gasping for release. I played Wynter's voice over and over in my head "Do you trust me?" She had no idea how she had saved me up until now, but this was her biggest task yet, what If she couldn't pull it off? What if she decided it was too risky and chickened out? No, she promised, she had never broken a promise before, so I clung to that promise, a symbol of freedom etched in my mind.

I didn't have very many memories of my earlier childhood, but one stood out, my father was at work, it was a warm spring day, the first day I had been brave enough to set foot outside. I remembered the garden seemed to stretch on endlessly, a sea of yellow daffodils and sunflowers, their faces pointing to the sun. I twirled around, dancing though them, my dress billowing like a dandelion puff caught in the breeze. I remembered spinning until the world blurred, I felt light and airy, like I could take flight, I closed my eyes and let myself fall into the bed of flowers, like I was one of them, wishing I was one of them, I remembered feeling happy, an emotion I hadn't remembered feeling before.

"What did I tell you about going outside?" My daydream was interrupted as my father snatched me back into the house. It was the moment I realised I could never be truly happy again, but then I met Wynter and that all changed, I found a whole new hope, and I wasn't going to let that go again.

I breathed a heavy sigh of both fear and worry as the big hand hit the 12 and the little hand hit the 8, it was time, I placed the watch in the pocket of my dress and tiptoed towards the stairs, stopping every so often to listen for my father moving. So far so good, I began climbing the stairs, the basement door was shut, my first obstacle. I placed my hand on the icy golden handle and turned, pushing it, just enough for me to slide out, not giving it the opportunity to creak. I listened again, the TV roaring from the living room, I peaked in, he was passed out on the couch. "This might just work" I thought. I slid through the hall, my body pressed against the wall as if it was going to make me invisible, just a few more steps and I was at the door, just a few more steps and I was free, well, almost.

WYNTER

"Alright, we're here..."
Stephanie got out of the car and opened my door, I stayed put, my eyes fixed on the seat in front of me, I closed my eyes and thought about Alma and Cleo, were they safe? Were they crying? What was going to happen to them? The tears stung my eyes, I never cried, Stephanie crouched down beside me and placed her hand over mine that were placed rigidly on my lap.

"They're nice people Wynter..."
"When will I get to see my sisters again?"
"Soon, I promise, this is only temporary..."

I knew she was just trying to pacify me, that she didn't really know what was going to happen, but I nodded and unbuckled my seatbelt. The house was big, way bigger than any house I had ever seen, it was two stories, one more than mine, the outside of the house stood like a sentinel, guarding secrets within its own weathered walls, it wore its age with grace, the brick facade, a patchwork quilt of russet and ochre, I wondered what its walls had seen.

"Wynter, this is, Norma and Ian Foxbury and their daughter, Elise..."

The three people who stood before me were the portrait of perfection, dressed flawlessly in their brand new, clean clothing, their hair brushed through, their smiles, genuine.

"We are so pleased you're here love..." The woman, called Norma said, she had a whisper of grace, her hair, silver threaded, framed her face, her eyes were sky blue and kind looking. Ian stood tall, his salt and pepper beard trimmed neatly, his eyes were crinkled at the corner and smiled when he did. Elise looked about my age if not a little bit older, her hair was chestnut coloured and fell in waves down past her shoulders, she had freckles scattered evenly on each cheek and some on her nose. I wondered if she had ever known hardship.

The room they told me would be mine was bigger than my own living room. It had a bed, an actual bed, one that was big enough for 4 people. The walls were plain apart from a couple of art pieces and there was a giant sheepskin rug in the centre of the room.

"What do you think? We're new to all this, but this room has been ready for a while, waiting, and now it's yours for a little while…"

"I want to go home…"

"I know sweetie, and you will, this is just temporary."

Temporary, I was sick of that word. I had learned growing up that everything was temporary, my mother's boyfriends, her soberness, happiness, but also at the same time, nothing was, I had a family, I didn't need another one. I sat my bags that were prepacked for me when I got home down on the floor.

"We'll just leave you to it…" Stephanie said "I'll see you in a few days Wynter… Ian, Norma, can I speak with you in the kitchen?"

As the door was pulled closed, I realised for the first time ever, I was well and truly alone. I looked to the clock that was ticking a steady beat on the wall and suddenly remembered, through all the chaos, Violet, she would be waiting on me, I promised her, everything was falling apart and I didn't know how to fix it.

I was in Gainsville, two Villages over from my hometown of Sherwood, it was where all of the rich people lived, doctors, lawyers, that kind of thing, a far stretch from what I was used to. It would take me about 20 minutes to get to Violet's if I ran. I stuffed all of my supplies into a back pack, skipping rope, check, torch, check, black hoodie check, pillow check. The door to the room creaked open and Elise entered.

"Are you running away?"

I zipped up my back pack and shoved it under the bed.

"Not exactly…. You're not gonna tell are you?"

"No…" Elise sighed "sisters don't snitch, go, do what you need to do, I'll cover you…"

"Elise" I called as she began to leave "Thanks…"

"Go out the back way, they can't hear you leave that way…"

I swung my bag over my shoulder and crept down the stairs, Ian and Norma were in the kitchen, Elise gave me the thumbs up and I left through the back door.

Sprinting I made my way through Gainsville, past all the mansions with fancy cars parked in the driveway, through Oliveswood, the little fisherman's village that housed 1,000 people tops and the majority of them were fishermen and down into Willow creek, a slightly more upper class version of Sherwood, I was almost there, time check, it had just gone half past 8, the streets were engulfed in darkness, the only light being from the dull street lights and the silver moon. Then I saw it, the sign "WELCOME TO SHERWOOD", I was late but I wasn't *that* late. My brain was processing a million different thoughts, fear, adrenaline, worry, anger, I felt it all. All of a sudden, my feet drew me to a halt, before my brain even realised what was happening, they were taking me off route, in the direction of my home. I had to see her, I had to ask her why. What about Violet? I thought, it'll only take a moment. I could see her through the window, just sitting on the couch, not on the phone begging to get us back, not crying on the floor and throwing things with despair. I took a deep breath and entered the house, she didn't look up but she knew it was me, her hands were

clasped around a bottle of beet.
"Mama?"
"What are you doing here Wynter?"
"They took them, they took Cleo and Alma..."
"It's for the best..." She lifted the bottle to her mouth and downed the rest of it before tossing it onto the pile on the floor.
"What, so you're not going to fight for us, what happened I thought you were getting better...?"
My mother sighed, her face drawn in and pale with dark circles under both of her eyes. It was then that I realised that my mother had no intention of getting better, that she was just another disappointment in my life, that my sisters and I getting taken away, it was no one else's fault but hers.
"I hate you..." The words spat from my mouth like blades towards a target, but I meant it, I hated that I meant it, but I did.
"Wynter, please, you don't understand..."
Her breath smelled of a mixture of alcohol and cigarettes, it attacked my nostrils.
"And you're drinking again... What about the baby, what about my baby sister?" The words flew from my mouth like daggers, but my mother didn't even react, not even a quiver of the lip or a tear down the cheek, she really didn't care and I hated to admit it, but it hurt.
"Babe, you coming back in?"
A man I had never seen before appeared from her bedroom, I stood there frozen to the spot, gobsmacked, my mother put her head into her hands. The man was huge, ripped, like he spent all of his days lifting weights at the gym, his eyes were such a dark brown they were practically black and his stubble was perfectly trimmed.
"Who's this..." He moved towards me.

"Stay away from me..." I screamed "And mama, don't try to get us back, we don't want you..."

VIOLET

The air was cold as it touched my skin, gently caressing my bear arms and legs, I had been waiting, I had been waiting but Wynter hadn't come, she was late…. Had she forgot about me? Was she not coming? Did she just not care? I sat cross legged on the grass by the fence and wrapped my hands around the iron bars. Darkness had wrapped the world up in a comforting blanket, everyone was settling down for the night, everyone but me. I looked down at the watch, the big hand was now at the 1 and the little hand at the 9 which was over a whole rotation late, I began to worry, Wynter would never let me down. I rose to my feet, inspecting the fence, I took a few steps back before running forward, as fast as I could, I jumped, gripping onto the bars but I didn't get enough height and I slipped back down, falling back onto the grass. The stars were out that night, I looked up clasped my hands and wished.

"Please, take me home."

I laid back onto the uncut grass, feeling like I could disappear into the ground, closed my eyes and felt the green blades between my fingers, the light at the end of the tunnel becoming more clear, I knew if I didn't make it out now, I never would.

"Hey! What do you think you're doing?" My father emerged from inside the house, his fists clenched with fury, his brow furrowed with rage I sat up as he snatched me from my dream state, his hand gripped hard around my wrist. "You have no respect for the rules!" As he yanked me to my feet, Wynters watch flew from my hand into the nights abyss, if she did come, she'd never get me out now.

Every single moments I spent with Wynter played over and over in my mind as my father dragged me through the hall, down the stairs and into the basement, each moment seeming more and more like a distant memory as he chucked me onto the cold floor, with every kick I remembered everything she had done for me and I worried for her safety, what if she showed up now? What if he caught her too? Everything, I thought, was unwinding in front of my very eyes. I could taste the blood in my mouth but I pretended it was fresh bread, straight from the oven, that I had baked with my mother, I could feel the bruises forming but I pretended it was a result of roughhousing with my sisters and then it all went black.

I was sure I had died as I came to, my body aching, I tried to stand but I couldn't, my bones felt far too weak.

"I really don't want to discipline you, Violet, you just keep on leaving me no choice..."
I turned my head as I lay curled up on the concrete floor of the basement, my father was sitting on my mattress. He had something in his hands but my vision was blurred so I couldn't tell what it was.

"You're disobedient..." He continued "Ungrateful and you can't be trusted..." He stood up, crouching down next to where I was lying. "What's this huh? And where did you get it?"
He forced the pieces of paper into my hand and I immediately knew what it was, I heaved my heavy bones up to the seating position.

"I know everything..." I ran my tongue over my teeth to make sure they were all still there. "I know what you did"
My father shook his head, standing up so he was now towering over me.

"You know nothing!" He yelled, his booming voice,

echoing off the walls. "They didn't want you, otherwise they wouldn't have left you out in the front garden on your own, at 3 years old, they were careless, irresponsible, they didn't deserve to be parents…"

"And you do?" I said, my voice in a whisper.

"Where did you get this?" He waved the pieces of paper around, making me feel nauseous with his movement.

"I found it…" I lied

"Liar!"

"Please, you have to tell me how it happened… I need to know, please…"

My father sighed, sitting on the ground next to me, he told me how at that time he had been lonely, he needed someone to keep him company, someone who wouldn't be a bother and who wouldn't fight back, someone vulnerable, like me. He spent weeks, scouting the streets for the perfect companion, that's when he saw me, I was walking with my father and sister from the park, he told me how he followed us to our home, how at first, it was my sister he wanted but he soon found out that she was too old, too strong, he needed someone weak, more compliant. For the next few days he watched my family, like a lion hunting his pray. He knew when we woke up in the morning, when we went to sleep, our daily routine. One Sunday morning, he watched my dad leave with my sister to take her to karate, it was just me and my mother, home alone. He watched as my mother sat me down on the grass in the front garden and scattered toys onto a blanket before sitting me down on the blanket as well and she began to garden. He watched as she planted flowers into pots by the door, every so often turning around to check on me as I was happily playing with my dolls, he said I was beautiful, like a porcelain doll. He told me how a few moments later, he heard the phone ring inside the house, he watched as my mother made the split second decision that would change both her and my life forever and she left me alone in the garden, that's when he pounced, driving until he was adjacent to where I was playing, springing from the car and grabbing me. He told me how, as I cried he drove to the end of the street and watched as my mother frantically searched for me, screaming my name. "Emily! Emily!"

"If my name is Emily, why am I called Violet?" I questioned, my heart breaking with every detail he added.

"It's what they called you, in the papers, the girl in the Violet dress, figured it fit…"

"You're a monster! I hate you, and you'll never be my real father!" The tears cascaded down my cheeks like water falls, the pain I felt inside my chest prominent but as the words left my mouth I knew I had made a big mistake…

My father grabbed me to my feet, the agony, coursing through my veins, I let out a pain fuelled yelp.

"You're going to wish you never said that."

He removed the rug from the floor that was covering my confinement and opened the trap door, dropping me in like a fish into the water.

"Please, I'm sorry, don't do this!"

"It's too late…"

The door slammed shut and I heard the rug sliding back into its place. All hope of escape was gone. All hope of being found was gone. All hope, was gone.

WYNTER

It was 9:30 PM by the time I finally reached Violet's and she was nowhere to be seen. Maybe she had lost hope when I didn't show up on time and had gone back inside? Every scenario that could have possibly played out, whizzed around my brain. If I said I was coming, Violet would have waited, what if she had been caught. Suddenly, my problems didn't seem so big anymore, all I wanted was to make sure Violet was safe. I raked through my bag and retrieved my skipping rope, swung it high so it caught onto the spindle at the top of the fence, grabbed the other end of the skipping rope and tugged to make sure it was secure. I then tied the rope around my waist and began to scale the fence, taking all my might to carry my own weight. When I reached the top, I quickly swung both legs over and dropped to the ground on the other side, feeling my knees buckle beneath me on impact but I stuck the landing, I smiled to myself, phase one, complete. As I began walking across the grass I felt something beneath my foot, as I moved my foot, seeing a glimmering speck, I realised, it was my watch, Violet had been here. I picked up the watch and stuffed it into my pocket. Looking at the house, there seemed to be no sign of life, all of the lights were out and the house had an aura of deathly silence around it, what if she wasn't even in there?

The front door was not locked, it wasn't even fully shut, I pushed it open, causing it to creak, hesitating before making my way inside, into the pitch-black abyss. It was eerily quiet and the feeling in the pit of my stomach intensified with the worry I had for Violet. I pressed on through the hallway my heart racing, the old wooden floorboards screeching underneath my weight. The air smelled of dampness and decay, the wallpaper was peeling away from the wall. As I slowly descended the staircase down to the basement, my mind raced, a million thoughts spinning around my brain. Was Violet injured? Or worse? Had he taken her elsewhere? Would I ever see her again? I was stopped in my tracks by a hand coming from behind me to cover my mouth.

"You just made this so easy for me..." A husky deep voice said from behind, it was him. I plunged my teeth into his palm and he let go with a pain filled grunt.

"Where is she?"

"I'll show you where she is..."

He grabbed hold of me around the waist, kicking, screaming and punching with all my might, but his strength was unmatched, he marched me the rest of the way down to the basement, removed the rug and opened the door to the underground, that's when I saw her, just lying there on the ground, not moving.

"I'll be back for you later you interfering little rats!"

He dropped me into the vault narrowly missing Violet as I fell.

"You'll never get away with this!" I screamed as he slammed the hatch. Phase two hadn't gone exactly as expected, but I was hoping phase three would, because if it didn't, we were never getting out.

Violet didn't move a muscle, her broken and bruised body huddled in the middle of the floor, her face pale, her eyes wide with fear, I sat down beside her, her breathing was shallow, barely even there, her legs twisted in an unnatural angle, my hand trembled as I placed it onto Violet's back, she didn't react, it was like she was in a trance.

"I'm so sorry Violet..." I whispered "This is all my fault..."

Violet twitched slightly under my hand, slowly turning her

head towards me, the light from the moonlight that was bleeding through the tiny window cascaded onto her face showing off her bruises, she was almost unrecognisable.

"It's not your fault Wynter..." She tried to push herself up to sitting but she was just too weak "I knew you'd come...."

Violet, who was once an example of vibrancy in a very dark world, was now a canvas of pain and despair, her emerald green eyes swollen almost shut, blood trickled from her lip that had split slightly, staining her pale complexion, her hair, matted, tangled and knotted, clung to her forehead, damp with sweat. Gently, I cradled Violet's delicate head, lifting it from the hard ground onto my lap, my heart clenching with concern, she flinched, her breath hitching and her body tensing. My resolve hardened, I had made the choice to survive and I would carry Violet over the finish line if it killed me, I took my jumper off and placed it underneath her head to cushion the hardened ground and rose to my feet, gripping the bars on the window in my fists I began to shake them vigorously until one came undone, I then tried to use the bar to unhook the latch on the door but it was no use, he had thought of everything, it was a fake latch, the door could not be opened from the inside. I sighed, throwing the bar against the wall with frustration, I sank to the seating position again. I didn't tell Violet but I had begun to get really worried that we may not make it out alive.

The minutes crawled by at snail pace, I could feel myself drifting off, but I was awakened by a slight commotion outside, I stood up and subtly peered through the window. He was outside, pacing back and forth on the grass, he seemed irritated, agitated and like he was on a mission. All of a sudden he crouched down at an area of the garden, placed his hand onto the grass and nodded, that's when he started digging, what was he digging for?

"Violet, you don't think he'd get rid of us, do you?"

"He's threatened to a few times…" She mumbled with laboured breaths, with trembling hands I helped Violet to sit up, she was like a dead weight, I placed my hands under her arms and dragged her so that she was propped up against the wall, but her head still slumped ever so slightly.

"You're stronger than you know Violet." I cradled her delicate head in my hands, her skin cold to the touch. "We'll get out of here, I promise…"

"What if this is it for me?"

"It isn't, think of your family, and how excited they'll be when they finally get to hold you in their arms…"

"What if I don't make it?"

"You can't think like that okay? You've got to be positive…"

Violet managed a weak smile, somehow she had grown more limp. How did we get here? How did this happen?

"Wynter, I'm cold…"

I picked up the jumper that I had placed on the ground for her to use as a pillow and draped it over her.

"Stay with me, okay Violet? Just a little bit longer…"

I reached into my bag and retrieved the flashlight that I had forgotten I had and turned it on to illuminate the darkness slightly, I propped it up against the wall. I thought about my mother, if she'd even care that I was gone, I thought about Alma and Cleo and about how I had to get out of here for them. I thought about what would happen after all of this? Would Violet and I remain like sisters? My thoughts were fizzing, I had exhausted every option of escape, maybe I just had to give in and realise I had failed.

PEYTON

In the evenings I mostly just went through the motions, feeding Penny, giving Penny a bath, getting her ready for bed. After she was in bed I would then, grab myself some dinner and sit down in front of the TV, but this particular night I decided to mark some of my class's work, I had set them an assignment to write about what they were doing at the weekend. I grabbed the folder that contained their notebooks and set up at my kitchen table. I wondered what wild stories I'd read, some of these kids had a very vivid imagination. Daniel Simon wrote about how he was going to a roller rink with his cousins but his mother had grounded him for teasing his little brother so he wasn't allowed to get pizza after. Martha Mayweather wrote about how her older sister Candace was taking her on a shopping spree and how they were both going to be picking out dresses for their Auntie's wedding. Genevieve Paxton went off on a 5 page spiel in true Genevieve fashion about how she was supposed to be going to Mexico for the weekend but her father had to work so her and her mother were just going to have a girly day on Saturday and they'd be going to Mexico next weekend and how on Sunday she Orla and Riley would be hanging out at Orla's house to watch movies and eat snacks, before I was finished, I shut the jotter over, my brain struggling to keep up with her words. I moved to the next jotter in the pack, Wynter Jones, I wondered what she had written about, I had heard about social work taking her away from her mother and sending her and her sisters to separate foster homes but I wondered what she hoped to be doing. I opened the notebook, what I read next changed everything.

Dear Miss Larkin,
If you are reading this it's either right on time, or too late... I've done something crazy, but it was for a friend, my friend Violet, only Violet isn't her name, it's Emily, Emily Myers, I don't know if that name rings any bells, but if it doesn't, long story short, she was kidnapped, 10 years ago and I need to get her out, the only way I could see how, was by going in... To get her, and with any luck in the world, I won't get caught, You might wonder why I didn't just go to the police as soon as I found out, well it's because, I didn't think anyone would believe me, so if you are reading this, I am probably in that house and we may both be in danger, I don't know the exact address but my address is 124 Credence Drive and it's the big scary looking one at the end of that row, please call for help, tell them it's urgent, we could be in trouble.
xoxo Wynter

The more I read, the harder I gripped the paged, my hands quivering, the words jumping off the pages like they were alive, was this all just one big joke? No, Wynter wouldn't do that, would she? I dropped the notebook onto the table and grabbed my laptop from the kitchen counter typing "Emily Myer" into the search engine, countless news articles appeared, "3 YEAR OLD STILL MISSING, POLICE HAVE PRESUMED DEAD", "KIDNAPPED EMILY MYERS WOULD BE 13 TODAY",

"EMILY MYERS MOTHER AND FATHER APPEAL FOR ANY WITNESSES WHO MAY HAVE SEEN HER DAUGHTER BEING TAKEN." I couldn't believe what I was reading, could this have been real, could Wynter have more weighing on her mind than just her home life?

I called the police at 11:10PM, after I had time to process what was going on and they said they'd send officers immediately and one to my home to collect the letter from Wynter, for evidence. At 11:20, I heard a knock at the door.

"Peyton Larkin? My name is Sargeant Olivia Hughes, I'm here about the letter..." A female police officer, no older than myself spoke softly as I opened the door. She was petite, no taller than 5ft, her uniform and equipment seemed heavy on her tiny frame. Her skin was cocoa coloured and her black hair was scraped back into a tight perfect bun. I invited her in and we both sat down at the kitchen table.

"It's from one of my students, I worry she might have gotten herself into some trouble, she's got a rough home life you see, so I am concerned she has no concept of danger..." I handed her the note and she inspected it carefully.

"And this girl, she wouldn't lie about something like this?"

"No..." I shook my head "It's too specific, how would she know?"

"Police have been looking for Emily Myers for 10 years, we really had lost hope, this could be huge..."

"Do you think Wynter is alright? The kid who wrote the letter..."

"it's hard to tell, we really don't know what we are dealing with yet, honestly, Wynter could be in imminent danger..."

"Sierra Hotel from control..." A voice sounded over

Olivia's radio, she unclipped it from her shirt pocket and raised it to her mouth.

"Go ahead…"

"It appears that Wynter Jones was filed as a missing person, she did not return to her foster parents after sneaking out, over…"

"Received…"

Olivia stood up, clipping her radio back onto her shirt pocket and filed Wynter's letter into a clear plastic bag.

"Thank you for all of your help Peyton, we will be in touch…"

"You'll let me know if Wynter is alright?"

"We will be sure to contact you."

VIOLET

My skin felt raw, as if there was no longer a protective barrier but only bruises and open wounds. The cold seeped straight through to my bones, gnawing what was left of me. The confinement hole was suffocating, a space too small for hope, only breeding sadness and pain. My chest felt tight, like every breath felt like a chore, I could taste a mixture of the damp earth and blood inside my mouth, my mind swirled with memories, meeting Wynter, Wynter teaching me how to read and now this. Wynter sat beside me, her head in her hands, she fought to save me, risked everything and more, but now we were both trapped. I turned my head to face her, my vision blurred but I longed for her to tell me it was going to be okay, even if it wasn't.

"Do you think we'll make it out of here?" I tried to catch my breath but every draw was a battle.

"I really don't know..." Wynter lifted her head from her hands, her expression mirroring my physical pain. Her hands were scraped and her clothing was slightly torn. "But I can have hope..."

Wynter reached for my hand and took it in hers, so gently but it meant something.

With every moment that passed my body grew weaker and weaker, like the life was draining slowly from my veins, I could barely hold my head up. Wynter's hand felt like a lifeline in my own, strong and unwavering.

"Just hold on for me Violet, okay?" Wynter's voice echoed in my ears. "Stay with..."

Suddenly my body felt light and weightless as if I was floating above myself, looking down on the broken shell of a person I had become. The bruises, the aches, they faded into obscurity, like I couldn't even feel them anymore, my mind wavered between consciousness and surrendering to the inevitable. Was I really about to fall at the finish line? When I had gotten so close? I fell into Wynter's embrace, her heartbeat echoing against my cheek. I could feel my breaths growing shallow, the edges of my vision darkening. I wondered if this is what it felt like, death, a gentle decent into oblivion, a light airy feeling, Wynter's warm embrace suddenly enveloped me in a cocoon of longing, that's when I felt it, freedom, my body went limp, my consciousness holding on by a mere thread, then I let go, slipping into the abyss.

WYNTER

"Violet, Violet, please stay with me, don't go…"
Violet remained in my arms as she drifted off, her skin pale and cold to the touch, I couldn't help but feel this was all my fault, if I had been here on time, this might not have happened, Violet might not have been broken beyond repair. I laid her down gently on the concrete and allowed myself to cry, tears stinging my eyes, I had no idea what to do so I just held her hand, hoping that she may feel it, my heart broke that I couldn't save her like I promised, I had let her down.

I hadn't realised it but I had drifted off, I was awakened by the sound of feet on the ground above us, had he come back to finish the job? I stayed, frozen to the spot, listening, the hushed voices above becoming more and more clear, could it be? We'd been found? I sprung to my feet and began banging the walls.
"Help! Please help us! Somebody please!"
The echo of my palms against the brick rumbled throughout the tiny room, scraping my skin until it bled. No one was coming no one could hear me, I could hear the commotion happening above but they couldn't hear me screaming, what if they never found us? What if we were stuck here forever?
"We're down here!"
What if it was a trap? What if it was him up there? Hoping that we made a fuss so that he could have a reason to dispose of us? I bit my lip and sat back down, listening as whoever was up there left, listening to our potential chance of escape disappear. My throat had become dry from all the yelling and I could no longer feel my hands.

I remembered the last time that I felt trapped, like a rat in a cage, I was 4 years old, my mother had left me alone to go out with her boyfriend of the week, at the time we lived in a measly little one bedroom apartment and the living room doubled up as my bedroom. She was gone for 3 days and I was too little to reach the shelves to get any food or drink, I lay in the middle of the floor, too weak to move until she returned, this reminded me slightly of that except then nobody relied on me but me and now, I had Violet counting on me, I didn't want to let her down, I wouldn't let her down, my sisters needed me, even my unborn baby sister, I had to get out for them. I stood up slowly and made my way over to the little window to look out, he was no longer there, all that was left was the spade he was carrying and a half-dug hole, I wished I could get inside his head, know his plans. That's when I heard it, the rustling of footsteps on the grass, I ducked down so that I could see out but no one out there could see me. Two sets of legs appeared in front of me, who were they? I remained paralysed with fear, my stomach twisting in knots inside me, I scanned from their feet, up their black trousers legs, I then realised who they were, they were the police, Miss Larkin must have called them, I thought, feeling myself smile with relief.

"No one is here boss…"

"Do a perimeter check…"

I cleared my throat, ready to speak but nothing would come out and they began to walk away.

"Down here…" I croaked, they didn't hear me, they were getting further and further away. "Down here"
The officer at the back turned his head to the sound of my voice.

"Boss, over here!"

The two police officers ran towards me and crouched down

in front of the window.

"What's your name kid?"

"I'm Wynter, Wynter Jones... You gotta help us, Violet... I mean, Emily, she's not in a good way"

"How do we get to you?"

I explained to the officers that they needed to go down to the basement, move the rug and open the latch on the circular door to the place Violet called Confinement. After they had disappeared from my view, I dropped to my knees and picked Violets lifeless body up onto my lap, stroking her hair with my hand.

"We're saved Violet, it's going to be okay!"

All of a sudden I heard it, the sound we had been waiting for and the door clambered open and I climbed up the ladders and fell into a female officers arms, she held me there for several moments. I watched as 2 paramedics climbed into the hole and began working on Violet, tearing her clothes from her body, pressing on her chest putting a face mask over her mouth, but Violet remained still, I clung to the officer, refusing to let go from fear it was all a dream and we were still down there.

"Come on sweetie, there's an ambulance just outside, they're gonna want to check you over..."

My feet were frozen to the spot, my eyes fixated on Violet, her tiny body pulsing as they tried to revive her, she wasn't out of the woods yet so I wasn't about to leave her. I dropped to my knees and crawled to the edge of the hole as close as I could get.

"Violet, please, don't leave me now, think of your family, don't you want to see your family?"

Finally, after several minutes, she gasped for air, it was the most wonderful sight I had seen, I breathed a sigh of relief and followed the female officer out to the ambulance.

As I sat in the entrance way to the ambulance being checked over by a paramedic I could see him, sitting in the back of a cop car, head down, not so tough now.

"You're a very brave young girl Wynter Jones, but next time, leave it to the professionals huh?"

The paramedic shone a light in my eyes, took my blood pressure and dressed my hands that were red raw, they also draped a blanket over my shoulders, it was a silent relief. Violet was stretchered out of the house, I ran to her side.

"Wynter..." She spoke softly "You kept your promise..."

I squeezed her hand as they bundled her into the ambulance and closed the doors before driving off. She was going to be okay, it was all going to be okay.

Violet

The entire way to the hospital I was drifting in and out of consciousness, until I suddenly fell into a deep slumber, when I awakened the world was blurry, the noise of beeping and Hussle bustle were playing in a symphony.

"Can we get a nurse in here, she's awake!"

My vision grew into focus, panic suddenly setting in, where was I and why did I have tubes attached to my body, was I dead?

"Emily, my name is Sargeant Olivia Hughes but you can call me Liv, I'm a police officer…"

I found myself staring, inspecting, I had never seen a real-life police officer before, was she here to arrest me? I sat up in the bed that I was lying in, it was more comfortable than the thin mattress I was used to in my basement room, and I removed the mask from my face.

"Where is my dress?" I asked, running my fingers over the gown I was now wearing, the texture rough and unforgiving.

"It got a bit ruined, but I promise, we can get you lots of new clothes okay?"

Another lady entered my room, she was an older lady, small in stature and plump with red rosy cheeks, she approached my bedside and began poking and prodding me and checking me over, I just wanted to retreat back into the bed out of her reach but it was no use.

"I want to go home…"

"Your family are on their way Emily…"

"No, back to where I came from…"

I could see the look of sympathy on Liv's face, her head tilting, her eyes widening.

"you're in the best place, they're going to help you here…"

"I want Wynter…"

"Wynter's foster parents picked her up and took her back home…" She paused, pursing her lips "Emily, you know no one here is going to hurt you right?"

"Stop calling me that, my name is Violet!"
I turned over onto my side and began to cry, but she didn't see me, I didn't want anyone to see me cry.

After I had settled myself, eaten the buttcred toast they had made me and relaxed a little, Liv told me, if I was ready I could meet my family. She said she'd stay with me the whole time, I had butterflies in my stomach, doing back flips, I wasn't ready but I was ready. All of a sudden the door opened and a man and a woman appeared, they looked different than I had imagined. The man was tall, slender but fit, he had an aura of wisdom and experience about him, his brown eyes held depth within them like he had been forced to age much quicker than he would have liked, his hair was thick and curly and sat neatly on his head. He dressed somewhat unconventional with his tweed jacket bearing elbow patches paired with a pair of faded jeans and worn-out white trainers, I could see he had tears in his eyes. The woman was slight, like she rarely ever ate, her hair was a light blonde, most likely dyed and tied into a messy low ponytail, she had lines on her face that told stories of woe. The approached tentatively, like I was a caged animal, like I might bite.

"Is that really her, is that our Emily?" The man spoke like I wasn't there. The woman began to break down, approaching my bedside and inspecting me with her beady blue eyes.

"After all these years, you still look the same, still beautiful…"
After all these years of not knowing the truth, I finally had a family, but for some reason I couldn't speak, I couldn't move, these people were strangers to me and I didn't know what to say.

"Your sisters are just outside, do you want to see them?"

I nodded, the man who claimed to be my father left the room and came back with two girls, an older girl whom he called Eleanor and a younger girl called Erica. Eleanor was athletic looking, dawning bright pink yoga leggings and a black tank top, her skin was significantly more tanned than the rest of the family and she wore makeup, she was a pretty girl with dark brown hair with a pink streak in it and the darkest of brown eyes that seemed somewhat heavy. Erica had big sapphire blue dough eyes, and a cluster of freckles on each cheek and some on her nose, her hair hung in ringlets down to her shoulders, she still had that baby face that eventually everyone grew out of, she bounded up to the bed and swung her arms around me.

"Erica be careful…"

"No, no, it's okay…"

I tightened my embrace on her, suddenly feeling normal for the first time since waking up. It was the most beautiful moment, I breathed a sigh of relief closed my eyes and just let go.

PEYTON

When Wynter didn't show up to school on the Monday morning, worry took hold of me, I spent the entire day wondering if she was safe, where she was, how she was.

"Pey, hey, are you alright?" I hadn't realised it, but I had been day dreaming, the pasta I was eating for my lunch had gotten stone cold, I set it down to the side as Lara sat down next to me, a look of concern on her face.

"Yeah, it's just been a rough weekend..."

"Yeah, I bet, is there anything I can do?"

I shook my head, wrapping my hands around my coffee mug, I lifted it to my lips and sipped.

"I'm really worried about her Lara, this is a whole lot for a kid to handle..."

"I'm sure she has the best people around her now..."

Lara placed a comforting hand on my back, I thought about the moment I decided to be a teacher, I was a shy nine year old who rarely stood up for myself and I had been receiving some grief from a couple of girls in my class, one day they were really fired up, harassing me in the playground, pushing me, calling me names, I ran inside and bumped into my teacher Mrs Collins, she was a sweet older lady with curly white coloured hair and horn-rimmed glasses, she took me into her class, made me a cup of tea and I opened up to her, she told me any time I needed it I could come to her classroom and have some time out, she was amazing, she made it look so easy, I had no idea it would be this hard.

As soon as the school bell rang and my students had left, I grabbed my handbag and headed for the door. I picked Penny up from the child minder, got in my car and drove, I had to see her, I had to be sure she was okay. I had memorized the address of her foster home from her file, It was in a posh area with big houses with immaculate gardens, like she had always deserved. I could see her at the window as I drove up, her forehead pressed against the glass, her expression heavy and filled with sadness, my heart broke for her. I walked up the driveway to the door, rang the doorbell and waited. A woman answered, seeming perplexed by my just showing up.

"Hello, my name is Peyton Larkin, I'm Wynter's teacher, she wasn't in school today and I am just checking to see if she is alright…"

"Is that in your job description?"

"Well, no, not exactly, look, I care about all the kids I teach but Wynter, she's a real special kid, she's not had an easy start in life but she always bounces back, I was just…"

"Oh come on in then…" She interrupted me, smiling the kindest smile I had ever seen.

She lead me through the hallway and into the living room, where Wynter was sitting on the Window sill, I knew she heard me come in but she didn't move a muscle, I sat on the arm of the couch next to her for a moment in silence with Penny sleeping in my arms.

"Wynter, your teacher is here to see you…" The woman announced before shrugging her shoulders and leaving us alone.

"I can't tell if what you did was incredibly brave or incredibly silly…" I joked, but sensing the tone I brought the humour back a bit "I know things have been really hard for you Wynter…"

"Everybody leaves," She pivoted her body around to face me, her skin stained with tears "My mother, my sisters, Violet, I'm sick of losing people…"

"I know nothing I can say will make it better but

things don't stay bad forever..."
Wynter stood up and sat down on the couch next to me, her head in her hands.

"I just wanted to save someone, because I knew I couldn't save my sisters, or my mother, so I wanted to save Violet, to prove I wasn't completely useless..."

"You're not useless, you're the bravest little girl I know..."

"Miss Larkin, will you do something for me?"

"Anything..."

"Will you please take me to see Violet in hospital? Please, I have to see her..."

"I dunno, I'm not sure that's such a good idea Wynter..."

Wynters foster mother re-entered the room.

"Wynter, we've already discussed this, your social worker doesn't think it is such a good idea for you to see your friend right now..."

I could see Wynters heart break, a look I had seen on her face a few times but she always tried to hide it, this time she couldn't. She rose to her feet abruptly and stormed out, slamming the door.

"Don't take it personally... Adjusting has been hard..." Her foster mother perked up.

I left Wynter feeling an emptiness in the pit of my stomach, wishing I could do something for her, longing for things to get better, I knew I could get in trouble for showing up to her house without good cause but I didn't care. I placed Penny into her car seat and got into my car just as the sun was going down and just sat in my car watching as the pinks and purples faded to black.

WYNTER

Journalists and news anchors swarmed my foster parents house as the news of mine and Violet's tail trickled out to the wider community, I had no idea how they found me but I didn't care, I couldn't think about that right now, I had to see Violet, I was worried she'd think I didn't care about her or I had forgotten about her. I laid on my back, staring at the ceiling, hoping an idea would come to me, I had to get out of here.

"They're here again..." Elise entered my room, closed the door and sat on the edge of my bed, she might just be my ticket out, I thought. I sprung up to the seating position, startling her and causing her to jump.

"Elise, you've gotta do me a favour..."

"Uh uh, no way, I am not covering for you again, look how well the last time turned out..."

"I'm still alive aren't I?"

"Wynter, seriously..."

"Please, I have to see her, I have to see Violet..."

"Fine, but I'm coming with you, my parents trust me, we'll just tell them we are going into town... But you get one hour..."

"Deal..." I smiled, it seemed like forever since I had done that.

Elise asked Norma and Ian if we could go to town to do some shopping, Ian agreed only if they could drop us off because they didn't want us getting caught up with all of the reporters and Norma gave us $20 between us to pick out "something nice", I hated lying to them but it was for a good cause. Ian drove us into the centre of Sherwood where all the good shops were, shops that I had never been able to afford anything from before, Elise and I waved as they drove off and high fived one another, success. We walked the 15-minute walk to the hospital, the same hospital Cleo was born in, I remembered that day well, I was stopped in my tracks as the memories came flooding back.

"You okay?" Elise asked, I nodded and we continued to walk. When we asked where Violet (Emily) was they told us ward 26, on the second floor, down the hall and the private room at the end, we made our way there, I could see her through the glass window in the door, she looked different, less pale, less sickly, less afraid. I stood for a moment, my hand pressed up against the door but for some reason, I couldn't open it.

"What's wrong?"

"What if she doesn't want to see me?"

"Oh no, you didn't drag me half way across town just to chicken out now…"

"I mean it Elise, what if this was a mistake?"

"Look, you'll never know, unless you try, so go, I'll wait out here…"

On Elise's advice I pushed open the door and entered the room, I hovered in the door way for a moment but Violet's smile invited me in further, she reached out her stick thin arms to me and I fell into her, it was like nothing had changed.

"I was starting to think you wouldn't come…"

"Yeah, I'm sorry about that, my foster parents have just been super protective because of everything…"

I sat with Violet listening to stories about her family how her mother made jewellery and had promised to show her how, how her father was funny, always pulling pranks and telling jokes about how her older sister Eleanor was a champion cross country runner and was on practically every team that there was and how her little sister was sweet, that she was the only one who didn't treat her like a breakable China doll. I was happy for Violet but I also felt a hint of envy, I hadn't seen my sisters since we were separated, my mother didn't care enough to straighten herself out to get her kids back and had yet again chose a man over us, and although I was surrounded by a lot of people who cared about me, I still felt so alone.

"I thought you've have brought Alma and Cleo with you, maybe next time?"

"Maybe…" I gulped hard, I didn't have the heart to tell her about what happened, she had been through so much I knew it would just break her heart.

"My mama said that you could come over any time you want, when I get out of here…"

"Really?"

"Of course Wynter, you're my hero…"

After an hour of chatting, laughing and catching up with Violet, we were interrupted, Violet's mother and father entered followed by a police officer.

"Emily, the police just want to ask you a few questions…"

"Mama, this is Wynter, she came to see me!" Violet's mother, tilted her head and softened to a smile, a welcoming smile, she opened her arms to me and enveloped me in a warm motherly embrace that I had never experienced before, I didn't want her to let go.

"Uh Wynter, police will want to speak to you too but we will speak to your parents about that…" The police officer announced, Violet's mother held me at arm's length and stared lovingly at me.

"Thank you Wynter, for bringing our baby home…"

Elise and I walked back to Sherwood town centre in silence, my brain was too full of thoughts, thoughts of the police wanting to question me, thoughts of that night circling round and round my brain, thoughts of life and what would have happened had I been born into a different family, it was true what they said, you can't choose the hand you are dealt. We sat down on a bench at the bus stop, waiting to be picked up when a familiar face approached me, that familiar face was Dominic.

"Wynter, hi..." He shuffled his feet nervously "I uh saw you in the paper, what you did for that girl was pretty courageous..."

"You were right about her Dominic, my mama, you only did what you did because you cared, I can see that now..."

"How are you doing, with everything?"

"I'm doing okay..."

"Good. Well uh, I'll see you around kiddo..."

"Bye Dominic..."

Just as Dominic walked away, Ian pulled up in his dark blue range rover to collect us from town. As we sat in the back of the car, Elise gripped my hand in a somewhat comforting way and didn't let go the whole way home and I knew it was to remind me that I was not alone.

VIOLET

The anxiety was bubbling up inside of me as I sat in bed, police officer in the chair in front of me, my mother and father standing by my bedside, all of a sudden the gravity of the situation had begun to weigh heavily on me, crushing my body with its bulk.

"Tell me about Marcus Avery?" The female police officer who had spent almost every day by my beside since I came to hospital broke the silence.

"Who?"

"The man who took you, Emily…"

"I didn't call him Marcus, I called him father, he told me he adopted me, that my own mother and father didn't want me, and I believed him for a while…"

"What was it like living with him?"

"Sometimes it was okay, if I followed the rules it was okay…"

"What were the rules?"

"Don't leave the house, don't come up when people were visiting, stay quiet, don't ask questions, that kind of thing…"

"And what would happen if you didn't follow these rules?"

I thought for a moment, my eyes widening with every memory, the beatings, the name calling, the hours and hours of cleaning guns and yard work in blistering hot weather, I could feel my body trembling, I was losing control, pulsing involuntarily, my mind racing, reliving every awful moment I'd ever gone through.

"Emily… Emily!" I could hear my mother calling but I couldn't respond "I think she's answered enough questions for today…"

Then it all went black.

When I came too I had no recollection of what happened, my mother got out of her seat and rushed to my side, taking my hand in hers, pain written all over her face, she stroked my cheek with her other hand, moving my hair behind my ear. I was so confused, I wanted to go back to the life I was used to, because it was all I had ever known but the life I was used to was what brought me here. I had missed out on so much of my life with my family that they were strangers to me, people I was blood related to but I had no connection with, it wasn't how I had dreamed it and I so wanted it to be. I wondered if they thought the same.

After two weeks in hospital I was discharged and taken home to my families modest little house, a banner pinned to the door saying "WELCOME HOME EMILY". I didn't feel like Emily though, Emily was a completely different person, I was Violet. My family's home was an old farmhouse that had been redone to make it more modern, the land went on for what seemed like miles and miles. Pink and red roses climbed the trellis that stood by the emerald green coloured door, their blooms nodding in the gentle breeze, A gnarled apple tree offered shade and vegetable patches were scattered over the garden. There was a swing set, slightly rusted but still sturdy. I wondered if it would ever feel like home, my father opened the car door for me and I stepped out, taking it all in.

"Come on Emily..." Little Erica grabbed my hand and dragged me inside excitedly.
As we stepped inside the large open kitchen offered to greet me with a mixture of smells, sunlight spilled through the lace curtains casting soft patterns on the worn wooden floor, there was a large loaf of homemade bread sitting on the counter. To the left of the kitchen was the living room, an old grandfather clock stood sentinel, its rhythmic ticking echoed throughout the whole room, the room was

filled with well used furniture, a sagging sofa with floral upholstery, a coffee table stacked with books and a stained coffee mug, the walls displayed family photos, showing that whilst I was gone, the world didn't just stop.

"Your home is beautiful…" I complimented as I gazed upon all of the sepia toned pictures.

"No Emily, our home… Come on I'll show you your bedroom. "

I followed my mother upstairs, Erica bouncing along beside us. Upstairs, my parents' bedroom boasted a patchwork quilt in all different colours of green, draped over the wooden bedframe, Eleanors room was the smallest room but apparently she wanted it that way, it was painted all white with medals hung on the wall from her various sports wins, Erica's room was like a unicorn threw up with pink walls and rainbow pictures and stuffed animals everywhere, then we got to my room, it was painted purple, a flowery duvet cloaking the bed, toys in every corner with a doll house the most beautiful doll house I had ever seen.

"We can redecorate for you, when you, were taken, we uh, just left your room as it was, in case you came back…"

"This is exactly what it looked like…?"

"Just how you left it."

I ran my fingers over the floral pictures on the wall and down the deep purple curtains, I wanted so badly to remember it, but I just couldn't, I sat down on my bed.

"I slept here?"

"Most nights, some nights you'd sneak into Eleanors room and sleep with her without us knowing until morning…" My mother picked up an old stuffed white bunny with purple patches on its arms and one ear and handed it to me. "This is bun bun, he was your favourite, you'd never go anywhere without him…"

I squeezed the soft centre of the bunny and held him to my chest, fleeting thoughts became heavy with the moments I had missed out on.

After my tour, I had begun to feel quite overwhelmed so my family left me to it, I laid in my bed, trying to gather my thoughts, bun bun lying on my chest, I wondered if I closed my eyes, I could wish and change the way things happened, I blinked hard, nothing, I closed my eyes again and opened them moments later, still nothing.

"I'm heading out to get a few groceries for dinner tonight, do you want to come with?" Eleanor, stood in my doorway, she wasn't as forthcoming as Erica, she was more withdrawn, moody, if you will. I sat up in my bed.

"on the way, could you take me to see a friend?" I had to see Wynter, she was like a lifeline for me, someone who understood, she was the only person who ever understood and listened without wanting anything in return, we were like kindred spirits and I wanted to keep her in my life as long as I had breath in my lungs.

"If you know where your friend lives, then sure..."

I didn't know her address but I knew roughly where Wynters home was located. Eleanor drove in silence, chewing gum and blowing bubbles, I watched as the world whizzed by, a blur of colours through the window. After describing the area to Eleanor before she started driving she seemed to know where she was headed. I had excitement bubbling up in me, it was the first time I would see Wynter and be completely free.

"It's that house there?" Eleanor drew up outside Wynter's house, it seemed derelict, unloved.

"I'll come back and get you after my grocery run..."

I nodded getting out the car, I waved her off before walking up the path to the door and knocking it, as my fist touched it the door swung open.

"Wynter?! Wynter?!" My voice echoed throughout the virtually empty rooms, maybe they had just gone out for a bit, I sat on the doorstep for what seemed like an eternity before anyone showed up, it was Wynters mother, I rose to my feet.

"Hi, is Wynter home?"

"No." She scoffed, a familiar smell came from her breath that was strong enough to knock someone out. "She don't live here no more…" She reached into her pocket, pulled out a cigarette, placed it in her mouth and lit it up.

"Where does she live?"

"How should I know?"

Wynter's mother stumbled off into the house and slammed the door, I sat back down on the door step and put my head in my hands when I felt a hand gently fall onto my shoulder, Eleanor had returned to collect me and she had seen the whole thing.

"She isn't here…" I sobbed

"Come on Em, let's go home…"

As she tried to help me up I felt myself collapse into her arms, a sense of hysteria radiating from deep within. She held me whilst I cried, wondering, if Wynter wasn't here, then where was she? Would I ever see her again?

WYNTER

Despite the fact I had given my statement to the police the night of Violet's rescue, I had been asked to go down to the police station to go over it again. Norma drove me and Elise came for moral support. The police station was a daunting place, I remembered being 7 years old and waiting here for my mother to pick me up since she had left me and Alma who was 2 years old alone in a bar whilst she went off with a man. I was taken into a back room with two officers and Norma, Elise waited outside.

"Is this where you interview the criminals?" I asked with genuine curiosity.

"I guess so, but those are few and far between in Sherwood..." The male officer with no hair and big round glasses told me as we sat down Norma and I on one side and the two officers on the other.

"Now, I know we have already been over this but we just want to make sure we get the correct information..."

I nodded suddenly feeling nervous, getting distracted by the spinning ceiling fan, spinning and spinning just like my brain was.

"Wynter, how do you know Emily Myers?"

"Well, I know her as Violet, I met her one night, she was sitting on the other side of the fence..."

"Were you aware of her situation then?"

"No, but neither was she, I found out about it on the 10 year anniversary, I just thought her dad was really strict, turns out he wasn't even her dad..."

I fiddled with the side of the table to calm my nerves.

"You're doing really well Wynter, this is helpful..."

"When was the first time you came into contact with Marcus Avery?"

"He showed up to my school, he was talking to my sister, Alma, he'd been watching us but my first real contact was the night I had planned on breaking Violet, I mean, Emily out, but things didn't exactly go to plan..."

"How so?"

I relayed every single moment of that night in detail, how I had come up with this elaborate plan but it hadn't worked out the way I wanted because the social worker took me to an emergency foster placement so I was late to meet Violet like we had planned, how I snuck into the house and found myself along with Violet forced into an underground bunker that he called confinement, how I thought Violet was dead and I thought that I would be next and how my plan had actually worked because my teacher called the police and how although I wished I had done things differently I was glad it had all seemed to work out, well, work out for everyone except me, I was still lost, nobody wanted me and everything was changing around me but I still remained the same.

"Thank you Wynter, that was really great stuff..." You didn't get anything after a police interview, like you got a lolly at the doctors and a sticker at the dentist, all you got was the empty feeling after it was finished.

"I have a surprise for you Wynter..." Norma told me from the driver's seat, beaming from ear to ear. "Your social workers have approved it..." The suspense was killing me. "You're going to see your sisters!"

I had an overwhelming sense of guilt for not protecting them and excitement for getting to see them again, but what if they didn't want to see me? What if they hated me? What if they blamed me? Norma parked the car at the side of a little fairytale-like cottage about 45 minutes from where we used to live, it was picturesque, like nothing I had ever seen, I wondered if they were happy here, I got out of the car tentatively, I could hear giggling coming from the back garden, I met with Stephanie and we made our way around to the back of the house where Alma was running around with a football on the grass, she was wearing all new clothes with a pristine hair styled in two pigtails, Cleo was sitting on the grass picking flowers from the ground, smiling, they were both smiling.

"Wynter!" Alma caught a glimpse of me and came hurtling over at full speed giving me the biggest hug in the world, nearly knocking me over. "I've missed you so much!"

"I've missed you too Alma..."

"Wynter, come meet our dog, his name is Sully!" Alma dragged me by the hand to the other side of the enormous garden to meet a black labrador that quite frankly stank but was very cute.
I lifted Cleo up onto my hip but she wriggled out of my grasp longing to be back down on the ground, I worried, I wasn't needed anymore.

"Hi, I'm Sophie and this is my husband Jimmy... Your sisters are just darling..."
Sophie was a redhead, just like Cleo, they looked like they could be mother and daughter, she stood with an elegant Pois, her fiery hair cascading down like autumn leaves caught in the gentle breeze, her skin was porcelain pale, a beautiful contrast to her red hair, creating a beautiful canvas for a cluster of freckles, her eyes, framed by delicate lashes were the colour of mossy forests, her lips, a soft rosebud pink curved into a thoughtful smile. Her husband Jimmy, wrapped his arm around her waist, he gave off hippie vibes, with his long, dusky blonde hair and bright coloured Hawaiian shirt, he seemed cheeky, like he would be fun to be around. I offered them both a smile.

"You can come see them anytime you like Wynter, Alma talks about you all the time..."

"When will we be back together again?" I asked

Stephanie who seemed uncomfortable by the question.

"Wynter..." She hesitated "This is how it is going to be from now on, like Sophie said, you can come and visit any time you like but your mother has signed over her parental rights and Cleo and Alma's fathers are unable to take them in so the Wilson's will be looking to take Cleo and Alma in on a more permanent basis..."

It was like a knife had been stabbed deep into my chest and twisted for effect, like the lights had been turned off in my world leaving me alone in darkness, like my whole life I had worked tirelessly to keep my family together and it had all be ripped away from me.

I was quiet the whole way home, I didn't say a word at dinner and when 7PM rolled around I closed the door of my bedroom and stayed in there for the rest of the night. There was a gentle knock at my door and then it creaked open, Norma poked her head around the door.

"Can I come in?"

I nodded and she entered the room, sitting down on the edge of my bed.

"I'm so sorry Wynter..." She spoke softly "life really isn't fair sometimes..."

"I'm used to it."

I lay facing the wall, my arms folded over my chest, fighting back the tears that were welling up in my eyes.

"I know I'm not your real mother, but you can talk to me about anything..."

"I rarely could talk to mama about anything..."

"It's okay to be sad, you don't always have to be strong..."

"No one needs me anymore, Alma and Cleo have their new family, Violet has her family, no one needs me..."

"that's not true, you saved Violet's life Wynter, if it wasn't for you, she'd still be there and as for your sisters,

just because you don't have to mother them anymore, doesn't mean they don't need you..."
I sat up, turning to face Norma.

"You really think so?"

"I know so..."

A vibrating sound came from Norma's pocket, she rolled her eyes and retrieved her phone from her jeans pocket, she held it to her ear.

"Hello, oh, hi Stephanie, what's up? Oh my God, is she okay? Yes I'll let her know." Tentatively she placed her phone down on the bed taking both of my hands in hers. "Wynter, your mama went into early labour this morning..."

"What, it's not time!"

"She's fine, and so is your baby sister..."

After much pleading and begging Norma had been worn down and had decided to take me to the hospital to see my mother and new baby sister. I had butterflies in my stomach, both nerves and excitement, nerves about seeing my mother again, I hadn't seen her since I told her not to try and get us back, maybe that was why she signed her rights over and excitement to meet my new baby sister knowing that she'd potentially have a much easier start in life. Norma parked the car in the hospital carpark but I couldn't bring myself to get out of the car.

"C'mon Wynter, let's go..."

"I can't"

"Of course you can..."

"No, I can't do it..."

"I did not drive you down here, risking getting in trouble with social work, just for you to back out now, what's really going on?"

"I don't know if I can see her again... She was a crappy mama..."

"There must have been some good times..."

I thought for a moment, they were few and far between but we did have some good memories.

"There was…" I felt myself smiling "We watched the nutcracker together sometimes, I didn't like it, but it was her favourite…"

"See, now come on, you can do it…"

I could see her through the window of the door, she looked tired, she didn't really look like my mother. I caught her eye and for a moment we stared at each other through the glass. I placed the palm of the hand on the door, took a deep breath and pushed.

"Hi mama…" I slowly and tentatively made my way into the room, stopping at the end of her bed, she didn't take her eyes off of me. "Is this her?"
To the left of my mother's bed was a cot and inside was a baby, swaddled in a white blanket and a white hat, she was sleeping peacefully, I peered over at her, she looked just like Alma when she was a baby, I reached my hand down into the cot and caressed the side of her smooth cheek, she stirred but didn't wake up, I wondered what she was dreaming about, if she was even dreaming at all.

"You shouldn't be here…" My mother perked up, playing with the buttons on her hospital gown. "Really Wynter, you have to go…"

"Mama please, please, I had to see her, you at least have to give me that…"
With tears in her eyes, my mother nodded her head, her hands were shaking, I moved closer to her side and placed my hand onto hers, I didn't hate her, she just needed help, she offered me a weak smile, a grateful smile.

"What's her name?"

"She doesn't have one, the state are taking her away, she doesn't belong to me…"
I saw her begin to break and for the first time, I saw her as human.

VIOLET

Th dolls in my dollhouse, didn't get to choose their destiny, I did, I got to choose their names, I got to choose their stories, who they loved, who they hated, I got to choose everything about them. The dolls in my dollhouse were just like me, it felt like someone else was always pulling the strings, someone else was writing my story for me because if I was writing my own story, I would have written it very differently. I wanted to see Wynter but I had no way of contacting her and I had no idea where she was.

"Emily can I play?" Erica came bouncing into my room like a bouncy ball.

"I'm not playing right now Erica..."

"Sure looks like you're playing..."

"Well I'm not..."

I watched as Erica's face went from cheerful to sad in the space of 2 seconds and I couldn't believe that I was the cause of it, but I couldn't help it, everything hurt and I don't mean physically, my brain was hurting, my heart was hurting and I didn't know how to stop it. Erica walked away, her shoulders slumped, her smile faded and headed down the hall. I picked up the female doll from my dollhouse and threw it at the wall, causing the head to fall off, I then took the male doll, staring down at it, I could see his face, big and frowning, "Not so big now." I thought to myself before dropping it to the floor and stepping on it, I heard the crunch beneath my foot, it was satisfying, but it didn't make me feel any better.

When darkness fell, I was still awake, sitting by my window, gazing at the moon and the stars, I knew I was expected to feel at home here, like I'd never been away, but I just didn't feel like that, I felt like a stranger, like I didn't belong, my mother tried so hard, tried to include me, tried to make me feel like part of the family, my father was awkward, like he didn't know what to say or do, like he was lost, my older sister Eleanor, half the time I thought she hated me, the other half she merely tolerated me, my little sister Erica, she was a gem, but she didn't understand, she was young and naïve, she was my age when I was Taken, a part of me was jealous of her, she would get to be the child I never was, and of course I would never wish what I went through on anyone, but I also didn't wish it on myself.

"Lights out Emily…"
I turned my bedroom lights out and sat in the darkness, alone with my thoughts.

I woke up at the crack of dawn from a nightmare that shook me to the very core, I was back there, in the confinement, everything I had ever known and loved slipping away, it was then I had a thought, the only way I was going to feel better was if I faced my feelings head on. I rose abruptly from my bed, packed a few belongings into a backpack, snuck out of my room and down the stairs and out the side door. "What would Wynter do?" I thought as I headed for the road wearing only my night dress. It would be a long walk but I didn't have any money for the bus so I walked and walked and walked and as I did I thought about being really young, what I would have been like if life was normal? What kind of kid I would have been, would I have been funny? Serious? Quirky? I'd never know. The gravel of the road felt rough beneath my feet and the brisk morning air chilled me to the bone but for some reason, it felt normal.

"Violet! Hi!" A voice called from behind, a voice I recognised but couldn't put my finger on, I turned around to find it was Wynter's friend Genevieve.

"HI!"

"Wynter told me about what happened to you and I read about it online, I'm sorry that happened to you…"

"It's fine, it's all good now…"

"Where you off to in such a hurry?"

"No where really, hey, do you know where Wynter is?"

"No, haven't seen her in a while, last I heard she was sent to a foster placement, that's what my mama said anyway, but I'm not sure where it is and she's not been in school… I'll tell her you were looking for her if I see her…"

"Yeah, that would be great… Thanks"

Genevieve walked with me down the road, she was on her way to school, Genevieve talked a lot, mostly about boys and clothes, kind of like a budgie, if budgies were into boys and clothes.

"Must be great being back home with your family…" Genevieve suggested.

"Yeah, it's been great, really great…"

"Well this is me…" She said as we stood at the gates of her school, the same gates where Alma could have been kidnapped, I shuddered remembering the look on his face, the longing to get what he wanted. I watched as Genevieve walked through the gates as I stood outside of them before I continued on.

WYNTER

        I had never felt more a part of a family than I did with Ian, Norma and Elise, there was never any yelling, not a drop of alcohol in sight and Elise and I got on like a house on fire but it was time for me to go back to school, after much deliberation on what school I'd go, whether I would go to Elise's or not, but we finally decided to not upset the apple cart and I'd go back to my old school, where my friends were, where I felt the most normal. Ian dropped me off that morning, I had never been dropped off before, I waved to him from the gate as he drove off and headed though the playground to class where Miss Larkin was already seated at her desk.

    "Wynter, you're early…" She smiled sweetly. I owed a lot to Miss Larkin, she stood up for me when no one else did and she pretty much saved my life, I sat down at my desk got out my new pencil case and pencils that Norma had bought me and waited for the bell to ring. Once it did my peers all crammed through the classroom door like a bunch of animals escaped from the zoo.

    "Nice look Wynter…" Orla Grey commented I wasn't wearing anything particularly special but my hair was brushed and my clothes were clean, I looked like a brand-new shiny penny and I felt like one too.

    When recess rolled around Miss Larkin asked me to wait behind.

    "I'm glad you're doing well Wynter." She told me. "You really deserve it…"

    "Thanks for calling the cops, I was worried we would never get out of there…"

    "You're very welcome but I should be thanking you…"

    "You should?"

"Yes, I have never met anyone like you Wynter Jones, you always bounce back, you've taught me it doesn't matter how many times you fall, as long as you get back up every time."

"Well, you're welcome, I guess…"

"Alright, go enjoy the rest of your recess…"

I smiled nodded and went out to join my peers in the playground, Genevieve beckoned me to join her Riley and Orla, they were sitting on the grass discussing which boys were cute in our class, in my opinion none of them were but at least they were happy.

"Oh Wynter, Violet was looking for you today…"

"Violet? Where did you see Violet?"

"She was walking around this morning, looking for you…"

"I didn't even know she had been discharged…"

I lay back on the grass, the blades sticking into my skin like little pins, the sky was bright blue and there wasn't a sign of any clouds, I listened to the birds chirping happily, their tuneful melodies like music to my ears but my thoughts kept escaping me, back to Violet, back to the thought of her wandering around aimlessly alone looking for me, I shook myself out of it, maybe she wasn't alone, maybe she was fine, maybe, just maybe, I was over reacting.

Ian picked me up in the same place he had dropped me off, he had Elise with him in the front seat, I got into the back, he took us both to a quaint little ice cream parlour in town, one I always walked by but could never get anything from. Inside it was small, only the counter and the till could fit but the array of ice cream flavours was huge, so huge it overwhelmed me for a moment. Ian said we could have any flavour we wanted, my mouth gaped open at those very words and he just patted my shoulder and smiled. Elise ordered one scoop of cookies and cream and one scoop of chocolate with a flake stuck in the top and I finally decided on one scoop of bubble gum and one scoop of strawberry shortcake with sprinkles. Every mouthful was magical, like a party in my mouth, I had never had anything like this feeling before.

"Hungry Wynter?" Ian laughed as I scraped my tub of ice-cream clean.

"I've never had ice-cream before, it's amazing!"

"You've never had ice-cream before?"

I shook my head.

"Well Wynter, there is plenty more where that came from…" Ian ruffled my hair as we all got into the car to go home.

I was now having daily phone calls with Alma so as soon as I got home Norma handed me her phone and I took the call in the kitchen. Alma told me how Sophie and Jimmy took them to the farm and she saw a baby lamb being born and how it was the cutest thing in the world, she told me how Cleo was coming along well with her talking and could now say "apple" and "sheep", she also told me how she missed me and wished we could be together, I wished for that too but I was growing accustomed to how things were, I was finally able to be a kid and I enjoyed that but I did wish that I could experience that with my sisters by my side.

"Bye Alma, love you…"

"Love you too Wynter…"

After dinner Elise and I went out into the street to hang out with the neighbourhood kids, she took her bike and let me use her scooter. We rode up to the entrance to the Forrest, dumped our scooters and bikes and headed through the trees.

"This is our secret place…" Elise whispered to me as we made our way up the steep incline through the dirt and out the other side where there stood an abandoned shed, decorated with fairy lights, old furniture and multicoloured rugs. Elise took my hand and ran me inside.

"This is so cool!"

"no one was using the shed so we made it our own, we all added something, maybe one day you can add something too…"

We stayed at the converted shed until it got dark, just chatting and laughing and playing games.

"We should probably get going before dad comes looking for us…"

I didn't want to leave, I didn't want this day to end but as I knew very well, all good things came to an end.

There was an aura of negativity in the air when we got home. Ian and Norma were sitting together on the couch, like they were waiting for us to come home, when we walked through the door I could sense their nervous energy, Norma stood up and slowly walked towards me.

"Wynter, we just got off the phone with the police,,," She paused "Your friend Emily is missing?"

"missing?"

"They said she ran away from home?"

Ran away? Violet ran away, why would she run away, hadn't she been dreaming of the moment she was home with her real family?

"We have to find her…"

"Wynter, it's late, it's a school night, let's just let the police handle it…"

"No, she's my friend, I'm going to find her…"

PEYTON

A Violent knock at the door awakened Penny from her slumber causing her to scream at the top of her lungs. I picked her up from her crib and went to answer the door, who was knocking on my door at this hour? I opened it and there stood Wynter, a sadness written all over her face,

"Wynter, what are you doing here?"
I invited her in, placing Penny down in her play pen.
"Violet is missing…"
"Where are your foster parents?"
"They're in the car, please, Miss Larkin, will you help me?"
I knew I was breaking every rule in the book just having Wynter in my apartment, what more could I lose? I nodded in agreement, grabbed my coat and my daughter and headed for the door. Wynter had come up with the plan of splitting off into teams so cover more area, she and I would go door to door asking if people had seen her and Ian Norma and Elise would scour the town to see if she was lost or hurt anywhere. The police were also out in full force, searching bodies of water and fields, I tried to shield Wynter from that.

"Miss Larkin, do you think we'll find her?"
"I dunno, she wouldn't want to cause harm to herself, would she?"
"I don't think so…"
We had been to at least 15 doors to no avail, no one had seen her, no one knew where she would go. Could she have gotten a bus and left town? Wynter said she wasn't street wise enough for that, but a person doesn't just disappear. We took a short cut through the park, Wynter sighed before sitting down on a park bench.

"We'll find her..."

"This is all my fault, I have been so wrapped up in my own stuff, I didn't stop to think about how she felt, how hard it would be for her..."

"It's hard for both of you, Wynter..."
Penny had fallen asleep in my arms as we had walked through the streets, making cooing noises as she breathed in. I thought about how I would feel if it was Penny who was missing, it didn't bear thinking.

"C'mon, we're not going to find her sitting about here..." I nudged Wynter playfully with my elbow, causing her to break into a smile.

8 more houses, and nothing, we were both beginning to lose hope in the search but Wynter refused to give up, if she could stay out all night, she would.

WYNTER

My brain was unable to compute where Violet might have gone, we had been searching for hours, it was late, we were tired but I was unwilling to give up no matter how many times the adults around me urged me to. Miss Larkin had headed home to put her baby down to sleep so that just left myself, Ian, Norma Elise, Violet's parents and her older sister.

"It's like looking for a needle in a haystack…" Violet's mother sighed, her eyes red raw from all the tears she had cried. "What if we scared her? We just wanted to show her she was part of our family"

Violet's father placed a comforting arm around his wife and pulled her into a warm embrace, kissing her forehead. The police had decided to call off the search until first light, but we weren't going to give up. That's when I remembered the conversation I had with Genevieve about how Violet had been looking for me.

"I'll be back, I just have to talk to someone!" I began running full speed.

"Wynter?" I heard in the distance but I didn't stop. My legs were burning but I pushed them to keep moving, I refused to let Violet down again.

When I reached my destination, I knew I had to do things a little bit differently, it was late so I couldn't knock on the door. I picked up a pebble from the front garden and it threw it, it clinked off of the upstairs window, nothing, I picked up another pebble and did the same thing again, this time a light switched on from inside the house and the window sprung open.

"Wynter Jones, what the hell is wrong with you?" Genevieve exclaimed in a hushed tone, her hair sticking up like she had stuck her finger into a wall socket. I beckoned her to come down and waited by the door for her to make her way to me. Moments later the front door clicked open and she shut it behind her.

"It's about what you said earlier…"

"What did I say earlier?" Genevieve seemed puzzled but also half asleep.

"How Violet was just wandering around looking for me, well she's missing, and I need to find her, do you know where she was headed?"

"She's missing?"

"Yes, so I need to know what you know G…" Genevieve thought for a moment, she was dressed from head to toe in pink, pink silk pyjamas, pink fluffy slippers and a pale pink hoodie, she looked like a pink monster had thrown up on her.

"I know she was dressed in what looked like a night dress, she had a back pack and she was barefoot, she was acting all weird and when I asked her where she was going she said she was looking for you so she walked with me to school and then I went in and she waited outside the gates…" Genevieve paused "I didn't know she was running away, I just thought she was just being odd…"

"So you don't know where she went?"

"No, but I want to help!"

"What about your parents?"

"What they don't know won't hurt em…"

"You're a good friend G…"

"Oh wait, I have something for you?" Genevieve disappeared back through the front door for several moments, coming back with a white shopping bag, she handed me the bag.

"What's this for?"

"Just open it…"

I peeled open the bags opening, and pulled out an item of

clothing, it was the shorts I had been looking at the day that I found out about Violet being a kidnap victim, I couldn't believe she had gotten me them.

"I saw you looking at them, the day you bolted... So I got them for you..."

"thank you Genevieve..." I pulled her into a hug, she'd been a really good friend, especially this past little while, I owed her a lot.

"C'mon, let's go look for your friend..."

The beauty of the night was tainted by our worries for Violet. The silver moon sat high in the sky, all alone, not a single star up there with it, I wondered if Violet felt alone wherever she was. I thought about where I would go if I ran away, I'd go back to where I came from, where I grew up, that's it!"

"I know where she is!"

VIOLET

As I returned to the place that had once cradled my body in the darkest of nights, the world seemed to stand still, the trees blew in the gentle breeze, their gnarled branches reaching out as if trying to grab me. The path was overgrown, like it had always been, uncared for, unloved. As I walked down the path the grass welcomed me, grazing up against my ankles. I had a lot of memories here. My footsteps, hesitant as they were, had purpose, I was lost and desperate to find myself again.

The remnants of where I used to stay, unbeknownst to the world outside stood before me, a skeletal frame, its bricks weathered and derelict, I didn't remember it looking so run down. The walls inside once witnessed my cries into the night, they saw it all.

My breath hitched as I stepped inside, the memories all came rushing back to me as I wandered the halls, so much pain happened here but it still felt like home, the peeling wallpaper, the smell of damp and mould, the darkness. I traced my fingers along the shelves that were now bare. The floorboards creaked, as if echoing the ghosts of my past. I slowly descended the stairs to the basement, yellow police tape blocking it off, I ducked under it and continued on. It was almost exactly as I left it, I placed my bag down at the bottom of the stairs and sat myself down on the camp bed, the springs creaking on impact. Tracing my finger along my writing on the wall. If I stayed here forever, I'd never be a burden to anyone, not Wynter, not my parents, not my sisters, not anyone. I began to become a bit peckish so I grabbed my bag and I pulled out the packet of animal crackers I had stashed in there for a rainy day, it's all I had so it would have to do. Once I was finished my stomach growled for me, I was used to the growling so I ignored it.

The air seemed to hold its breath in this place, like it was keeping secrets, maybe it was. I closed my eyes, willing myself to remember, the taste of fear, the ache of hunger the chill of the icy cold, the wonder if there was a better life somewhere else. The rope that had clutched my ankle with its frayed grasp was no longer here but the weight still felt heavy on my heart like a phantom ache. I raised my face to the ceiling wondering if there was more to life than this, what had brought me back here? All this place had brought me was pain, why did I feel the need to punish myself? The doctors said I had great health for all I had been through, all I had been through? This was my life for 10 years and at the time, I hated the feelings of fear and anguish but now I missed it.

"Nobody wanted you, that's why I took you in…" That's what he used to say to me. "You're lucky you have me…"

I fell to my knees, the cold concrete beneath digging into my kneecaps.

"You're worthless, useless, nobody wants you around…"

I placed my hands over my ears, closing my eyes tight trying to block out the noise. I felt haunted, my brain haunted with thoughts.

"You're lucky I keep you around…"

Every sound felt like a threat, a bird chirping, the sounds of the wind battering against a window, I felt like I was in a minefield.

"Stop, stop, STOP!" I yelled into the air, knowing no one could hear me but all of a sudden the world fell silent, an eerily haunting silence.

I thought about my parents, if they missed me, if they'd just go on with their lives, about my sisters, they had each other, they didn't need me. I thought about Wynter, if she was okay, if she was safe. The watch she had given me had a broken face from the chaos of that night but it had sat by my bed my whole time in hospital and I wore it now.

"Wynter, can you hear me, where are you?" I whispered.

"I thought I would find you here..." A voice spoke softly out of the darkness. It was Wynter, she had never been more beautiful to me, like an angel, coming to rescue me, again. She walked slowly down the stairs, her face illuminating through every step from the moonshine.

"You're here, you're really here!" I jumped to my feet, suddenly summoning the energy and wrapped my arms around her in a warm embrace.

"I thought you'd left me..." I whispered as she held me, tightening my grip, I hoped that it wasn't all just a dream, that she was really here.

"I promised I'd save you, didn't I? I'll always save you Violet..."

WYNTER

As dawn broke, Violet and I remained in the old abandoned house sitting in the basement like old times but without the fear of getting caught, she sat chittering in her thin night dress and sockless feet, I handed her my jacket to wear.

"Why didn't you tell me about what happened with your sisters?"

"You had enough going on…"

"Wynter, I literally owe you my life… You can tell me anything…"

"You're right, I'm sorry, I should have told you… They're happy, happier than they've ever been, they don't need me anymore, I have a new baby sister but I will probably never see her"

Violet stood up, tracing her fingers across the concrete wall slowly.

"I thought that when I was rescued, when I saw my family again, it would all just click, like I had never been gone and when it didn't… I thought, it must be me, if I take myself away, maybe things will start to get better, then I thought of coming here, the last place I knew, the only place I really knew…"

"Did it work?"

Violet shook her head and slumped down against the wall in a crouching motion.

"Nothing in my life has been my choice, I just wanted to choose my own destiny, or something like that… Y'know….?"

"I understand, but running away is not the answer…"

"I didn't think I was running away, I thought I was running back…"

I stood up and sat down next to Violet pulling her in

towards me so that her head was on my shoulder, I could hear her heartbeat, loud and fast. I remembered the first time we met, how frail she looked, how small and lost, I could still see that girl in Violet now, and I felt like I always would.

"We should probably get you back to your parents huh? They've been going wild looking for you…"
"Wynter…?"
"Yeah?"
"Will you be in my life forever?"
"You can't get rid of me that easily…" I laughed helping her to her feet and we walked hand in hand out of the hell hole that changed both of our lives forever in both awful and amazing ways.

I bet you are wondering how this story ends, well stories like this don't really have an ending, life just goes on and on and on until it doesn't anymore, but I can tell you what happened next, Miss Larkin left Sherwood for a job in New York, she wanted to do something more with her life so she went back to school, got her masters in social work and went into that field, I like to think I inspired that one. Genevieve and I remained good friends, I still did her homework for her sometimes and she still paid me for it, until we got caught and her mother began paying me to tutor her. I never heard from my mother again, last I heard she was doing some jail time, something to do with drugs. My sisters Alma and Cleo were ultimately adopted by the Wilsons, Cleo learned to talk and was working on walking and Alma was taking ballet lessons and doing horse riding, we saw each other once a week and I got to be as involved in their lives as I wanted, they were thriving. Now for the best news yet, my baby sister who now had a name, "Hope", chosen by yours truly, had been taken in by Norma and Ian, they didn't want to tell me until it was all finalised but when they did, I cried, happy tears this time. Violet ran away a subsequent 17 more times before she finally settled, her parents sent her to therapy and after a year of home school she was sent to a public school, I saw her almost every day, we never did lose our bond and her, Elise Genevieve and I all became inseparable. As for me, Ian and Norma fostered me on a more permanent bases in the hope to adopt me and Hope and I decided that I wanted to become a teacher, like Miss Larkin, I wanted to change the world but there is something else, Violet taught me that no matter how many times you feel like the world has broken you, stand back up and show that you are resilient.

Printed in Great Britain
by Amazon